THE FACE OF INNOCENCE

THE FACE
OF INNOCENCE

By

William Sansom

THE REPRINT SOCIETY

LONDON

FIRST PUBLISHED 1951
THIS EDITION PUBLISHED BY THE REPRINT SOCIETY LTD
BY ARRANGEMENT WITH CHATTO & WINDUS
1954

PRINTED IN GREAT BRITAIN BY
T. AND A. CONSTABLE LTD
HOPETOUN STREET, EDINBURGH

I

'IT'S the Camberleys!'

And sure enough it would be.

Over many mid-Surrey lawns, green with summer and chalked for tennis—that cry would go up. In winter it would echo through the gelatined leaves at lounge windows and out on to the kempt yellow gravel of drives: 'It's the Camberleys!' And there indeed they would be, peering and waving, clicking busily the doors of the car, walking forward the two of them—Eve Camberley and Harry Camberley and as time was to go on the infant Miles Camberley.

The Camberleys were of "Uplands", Oxley Heath. To see them mothering their roomy saloon to a halt, Harry efficient and manly and politely attentive to Eve, Eve smiling and pretty and smart—to see those two come chatting and peering up the drive their friends would think: 'What a charming couple! Responsible young people—*and* cheerful too. Harry's got on well, Eve's fun. Theirs (if conditions don't get too much worse) is the future! They've got *everything*!'

However—

—It all began some four years ago, when I ran into Harry one day in the Strand.

'Why!' Harry said. 'If it isn't you, you old sonofer!'

'Harry! How *are* you?' We stood shaking hands, as always pleased to see each other.

'And what, may I ask, brings you to this part of the

world? Where's the Desk in deepest Chelsea? The Dressing-Gown? The smoke-fogged clatter of the Typewriter . . . or is it a Pen? A quill . . . what *do* you write on, by the way?'

'Brandy,' I said, as usual with desperate facility falling into his tone. Harry's tone of well-to-do facetion was more treacherous than most.

'In that case,' said Harry, 'let's adjourn.'

We went into a nearby bar. Then we started to work out when it was we had last met. There, with the neon paling a plate of almonds, with shadows of passing buses enlivening the watertank security of our glass doors and our stooled carpet, we found that it was at least six months. Heavens, we must see more of each other! Why didn't we meet more often?

Why indeed. That was very plain. We were old friends, very old friends, friends so old that we had lost interest in each other. Life had led us in different directions, the things we liked were now different, our acquaintances and our tastes had changed. All we had in common was a real lack of indifference towards each other. We had the past, and the past acted as strong as a bloodtie. We had been to school together. Later we had weaned our first manhood in close friendship. There was a conspiracy between us.

Such conspiracy had the effect of tolerance. It seemed that whatever either of us might do that probably bored to death the other, it was not met with disapproval; but instead with quite a warm indulgence. I used to feel: 'Well, well. It's only Harry. Old Harry.' And I would feel not at all guilty of my yawn, I would feel sure it was neither condemned nor even recorded.

Silence, after the first outburst of meeting, was easier between us than between newer friends.

Enduring the endless account of some escapade I had entirely forgotten, or tales of old faces I could no longer remember—I found myself unnaturally attentive. And as I listened I made excuses for him. And similarly I am sure that if Harry had been caught drinking with me by a business friend—Harry Camberley is a marine engineer—and afterwards that friend had commented disfavourably on my odd appearance—I cannot stop myself from time to time appearing in the accepted uniform of the artist—then Harry would have smiled and said: 'Yes, but you know I've known that chap years. Went to school together. Chap's a good fellow. Scribbler, you know.' To Harry I was always a 'scribbler'. And my books were 'tomes'. I don't think he has ever read, though he might have started, one of them: yet he has been pleased, both genuinely and because of its connection with himself, at what little reference to these works there has been in the press. But he would have felt much more proud if I had won an Old Boys' race.

So there we were discussing old times together. And even more recent times. Both bachelors, we sometimes took a giddy evening out together. Perhaps twice, three times a year. Usually we got comfortably drunk, and ended up pleasurably in a night-club. And so as we were talking I suddenly felt like that, and found myself saying:

'Look—what are you doing this evening? Or some evening this week? Why don't we meet and have dinner?'

We always called it 'having dinner'. He knew what

3

that meant. He planted his umbrella between his toes, looked down at it and laughed:

'No, old boy. Nothing like that these days. Not feasible.'

'But—that doesn't sound like my Mr. Camberley?'

'Come off it. You've got to remember who I am, old man.'

'And who in hell are you?'

'No no. This is a serious business.'

'And I'm suggesting we seriously go out.'

'And seriously the answer's in the negative, old man. Can't be did. We all come to it in the end. I've come to it, and there it is. Very nice, as a matter of fact, it is.'

'I'm sure it must be very nice. But do tell me first— what on earth *is* it?'

He laughed again, an oddly ashamed laugh for a provident bowler-hatted man with a moustache. He seemed to think I was making fun of him. And then abruptly his laugh left him, his eyes opened wide, and his face came up from the coy ferrule between his toes and stared at me in wonder.

'Good Lord!' he gasped. 'D'you mean to say you don't know?'

'Don't know *what*?'

His mouth was making a little circle of surprise— blowing out air, blowing out a plum. But then his surprise turned crafty—he realized he had the plum and that really I knew nothing of it. So he kept the look of surprise, widened his eyes and clowned it. It was done I am sure simply from a desire to please, he did not want to provoke excitement but wanted me to be excited and to like what he was going to say. But it took so long that I had to look down—and I remember very well an olive lying on the bar with its wooden stick

4

penetrated sharply right through, the little wooden
point emerged from the other side.

Then Harry's voice at last:

'Wait for it, wait for it, man! . . .'

He paused, and blew out a great breath:

'*I'm going to be married!*'

I looked up, trying to look startled. There was his
face still, exactly where it had been before. But now the
surprise had left it, he was beaming with his jaw
aggressively forward. He was twinkling hard into my
eyes to see what was there. There was not much.

To be honest—I did not altogether care. Yet there
was that face I knew so well—and in the next second I
did begin to feel glad that he was happy. But under-
lying this must have been much of the uneasiness with
which the news of a wedding is received. A feeling not
so sacred as it should be—a taste of stale champagne
muddled with a sensation that serious news has arrived
from the Front. Nevertheless—the loins must be girded,
the self must stand to attention and effect its grave
little message of congratulation:

'My dear Harry! I'm so glad! My *very* best congratulations!'

And then awkwardness made me add:

'And I suppose—to the most beautiful girl in the
world?'

Harry lowered his head gravely and repeated in a
cenotaph whisper:

'To the most beautiful girl in the world.'

A pause. Then:

'But let's drink to her! This calls for celebration!
A copious draught!'

He ordered two more of the same from the barman.

We were alone in that bar, it was still the middle of the morning and the presence of the barman there was embarrassing. He could not help overhearing. In his white impassive coat he was a figure of reticent authority. But he probably realized this too, he was nice enough to keep bobbing down behind the bar and shovelling about his glasses and his little trays of ice. So Harry ordered two more as it were from no-one, and soon these bobbed up. I waited a moment till the man again disappeared, and then asked:

'And who's the lucky victim?'

He looked grave. He said ponderously:

'Well, it's a girl I met.'

That seemed perhaps not unusual: but after a pause he told me how he had met her—Eve—about three months before. At some party. They had taken to each other instantly. There seemed, Harry said, to be no effort about it. It was from the very first easy and unanxious, just like talking to someone you had known all your life—yet there all the time in front of you was this face that simply took your breath away! To cut it short, they had gone out together once or twice: and then all the time. And a month later Harry knew she was the only one, he was deeply in love with her and this was the first time he had ever been in love and he had proposed and she had accepted even before the words were out of his mouth. It was the real thing.

I knew Harry very well and he had often come to me before, dog-eyed and moved deeply, with the 'real thing'. But one should always give this the grace of possibility. The real 'real thing' does come along. For whatever the reason, belief takes the air—and it is not impossible that this may for a lifetime remain un-

swayed. Harry apologized for talking in such detail—
but, as he always said to me, I was the only chap he
could really talk to. He knew I'd want to know something more about her. Well then—she was from the
country, making a career for herself in London. What
did she do? Oh, a lot of things. She had no precise
job, she didn't like to be too tied down. She worked
sometimes in exhibitions, demonstrating this or that.
Or perhaps helped with a show some Ministry was
putting on. Or she took small film parts. And she was
a model—not an artist's model, nothing like that. No,
a photographer's model. Fashions, advertisements, and
so forth. It was her idea that, by getting to know the
ins and outs of what was going on, she would be
learning all the time and eventually fall on her feet
into some responsible, some executive position. For
instance, Harry said, Interior Decoration.

At this I ordered more drinks quickly, and Harry
went on. He talked with reverence—and I stood there
watching his face and listening to the humble tone that
came from it, considerative and reverent and almost
apologetic. He had—if it does not sound too silly—a
round square face. That is, a square-boned face that
had grown round it a solid maturity of flesh. Yet it
was male and tough, it was not unlike one of those
faces you see in advertisements for men's clothes.
Indeed, somehow one always thought of Harry in an
overcoat. It was a distinguished, indistinct face. He
wore a reticent bristle of moustache—neither too long
and fierce, nor too trimmed and fastidious—a moustache that after a while became invisible. Had he, one
thought afterwards, a moustache? In all, his six-foot of
appearance came from a middle-class matrix designed

7

to provide the leaders of a new commercial aristocracy. He was also kind, patient, tolerant, blind as a bat to a great many things, and about forty years on.

But as I watched him he suddenly shot me a sharp blue glance that reminded me he was also shrewd: and his voice grew, despite the usuality of what it said, serious and definite:

'Of course, I know I'm taking on no chicken. I don't mean chicken—I don't know how old Eve is, in her mid-twenties I should say—no, I meant no plaster saint. That is, she may be. But she's seen a bit of life. She's not out of the cradle. She's been on her own a good while. She knows this sink of iniquity we live in, she knows the round of the town. And she's travelled a bit—knows the Continent. What I mean is she's had quite a life. I shouldn't be surprised if she hasn't had a chap or two after her before—but that's none of my business. I did hear something about her being engaged before—an airman. But that's neither here nor there. As far as I am concerned she starts from scratch.'

He raised his eyes and looked straight at me, in appeal, urgently:

'I love her so much, old man.'

Corners of the bar took my eyes, a steel chair with a red leather cover stood suddenly desperately alone. In the humming silence I began to stutter how very, very glad I was—when Harry suddenly swung his umbrella and gave a great deep chuckle. He raised his voice loud, not caring for anyone:

'God, I'm the luckiest man alive!'

Then he turned to the barman and told him to have a drink himself and hurry up with two more for us. Then he was talking fast at me again:

8

'But what a fool I am—you must *meet* her. Yes, you two must meet! What are you doing for lunch on Saturday? Come and have lunch? Going away?'

I was not. But I hesitated. I had known these great loves of Harry's before, I was trained to take them unseriously. But then—he had never before got engaged.

'I'd like to lunch very much. Saturday would be fine.'

We left soon after that, and I walked alone down into Trafalgar Square. There, in wide prospect, was the outside world again. The tall monument with its lonely figure, the black lions crouched moodily back to back, the toy escapade of red buses, the hundreds of people and hundreds of pigeons filling the pavements and the air with movement. Gone was the intimate magic of the bar. Harry's enthusiasm lost value as the world exposed its various purpose. The buildings asserted themselves—there to the right was Art, there a white palace of Empire, there great offices of Business, there the descent to Government. Harry's private world paled into perspective. I thought to myself, waiting on the kerb, wondering how to cross, working out the confusion of traffic lights and white lines and metal studs and islands and the dangerous stretches of skidding tarmac: 'Of course Harry's going to marry this girl. And I am of course to meet her. But—she will be a girl of Harry's choosing, not mine. Once again a strange partner will be thrust at one, a somebody gilded in a friend's eye by the illusion of love but to one's own eye stripped discourteously bare. A somebody whose faults are overlooked in the tolerance of love and whose virtues are forever exaggerated. O couples!'

But in this I was wrong.

II

THE FACE OF INNOCENCE

SATURDAY came, and at one o'clock I walked up the concrete path to the entrance of the flats where Harry Camberley lived.

It was a large block, red and towering, with windows set in forceful bands of horizontal glass. I passed into an inner courtyard—the traffic was muffled off, there was a padding of high walls round the ears. Sounds became intimate—a clatter of kitchen pans, a laugh from an open window, the creak of a window-cleaner's leather, the echo of a radio: on the sponge of turf centering the well, sound within those walls seemed curiously insulated—that radio would have sung too loud from the windows of an older house.

I found the porter's desk empty, worked out with difficulty from a simple arrangement of arrows and multiple numbers where Harry's flat was, took the lift up. At last, after walking blindly through a maze of corridors and dead-ends, I found the cream door with its illegible number. Harry was there immediately—he might have been waiting.

'Ha, the first arrival!'

He was primed with the buoyancy of hosts. My heart sank as I thought what fellow-engineers, what relatives or flat-friends might make up these other arrivals. I had thought the three of us would be alone. It is always a mistake to imagine beforehand what an occasion will be like, to let one's mind even lightly construct the look of a room and the people in it and—worst of all— the things one will say: it is a mistake to expect. Sometimes things turn out very much better, sometimes worse—but very often too they turn out much the same, only vastly different in detail, to the sort of picture one has made: then the jerky minutes reassembling the pieces in the puzzle, uneasy readjustment of the address before finally arriving.

As Harry ushered me into his sitting-room, I saw with relief that the dining alcove was laid for only three.

'Eve's late,' he said. 'However, the early bird—sherry, gin?'

But we had not time to say more before the doorbell gave its discreet carpeted burr. He put down his glass eagerly to go to the door and left me alone in the pale-wood pleasant room. Perhaps Harry had an engineer's eye for simple design, or perhaps he had bought the furnishing complete from a firm of good taste. In any case, here were delicacy and solidity in their right proportions: and comfort. Except that the clean pale body was scarred here and there with the indulgences of Harry's profession. I was just looking at a brass cigar-cutter made in the form of a ship's engine-room tele-graph—you put the cigar in a hole and abruptly jerked your craft from half-speed astern to full-speed ahead—when the muttering of voices from the hall brightened, the door opened, and Eve came in.

I do not exactly know what happens when one sets eyes on—not 'sees' but 'sets eyes on'—a person for the first time. For one is retreating in self-evasion at the same time as coming forward to pick out as much as possible in the shortest, the most flurried time. It is perhaps a guide to character whether naturally one stabs for the weaknesses or looks for some complement of beauty. I had tried not to expect too much of Eve. I had tried not to expect at all. Nevertheless my mind had whispered quite clearly what possibly she might be. A pleasant girl with sexless eyes and a tweedy nature? A bewildering small girl with little to say and a way of thinking inward that is often called 'mousey'? An ambitious girl of good looks and set face with several ideas of her own and only hers? A hearty girl of weak character whose weakness is to be strong always and get things moving? And so on . . . none too bad, none too good.

But I was wrong. Eve was none of these. She was very attractive indeed—beautiful. All women alter from day to day, just as they can take off or put on a few pounds of weight—and I was later to notice that she was not always as nearly perfect as then. But the first impact was startling.

My sherry hand gripped the more firmly—one must be on one's guard in the presence of beauty—and we were introduced and soon all talking about each other. Eve sat in the soft light halfway in the room, it took her cheekbones and pronounced them high and slender; her pale hair gleamed like fine fuse-wire, her lips smiled happily but came to rest with a slight downturn at each corner as though something was to be deprecated. But I will not try here to draw her face. I can only say that it was a kind of face I like—and leave you to fill in the features from your own preference. Only—not a face too formally perfect: this a little too long, this a little short . . . but in these slight distortions the less a mask, the more a face of attractive character. She sat with un-nonchalant ease. She seemed alert. She smoked with her right hand and held the left, with its ring, in a too casually prominent position. When she reached forward with her cigarette to the ashtray, her hand hovered at it, then withdrew a little and let the ash fall onto the carpet. What she said, and what we all said, were undistinguished phrases of a first meeting.

Harry was courteous as ever, it was appealing to see how his eyes watched all the time to see what he could do for us. He fetched us drinks singly when we wanted them, he offered cigarettes, it was he who produced a match—he seemed always to be up and down, hovering, smiling, in no nervous and irritating manner but just pleasantly attentive. He was determined to agree with what we said. When Eve told us how she had had to forgo her economical bus and once more take a taxi, and what a joy, an extra luxury, the modern taxis were—like riding at ease in one's own car, but so much less full — Harry smiled, nodded energetically, and said:

'Powerful smooth-running buses too.'

Yet a moment later when I ventured that there was much to be said for the older taxis, that they felt somehow more prepared for emergency, they had an elastic feeling, he was instantly with me:

'A lot to be said for them, they're rattlers but they know their way about . . .'

This was not said with the weak vacillation that sounds from it. It was more from a wish above all things for affability, something stronger than the meagre subject we discussed.

Thus far so good. We were unstrained and easily comfortable together. It was not until somewhere in the middle of lunch, when we were at that point when plates are finishing, when sauces congeal and the remaining vegetables are no longer hot—that Eve in such a brief silence made an uncomfortably leading remark. As some people cannot leave a relationship as simply a feeling but must try to define it, must infuse their verbal summing up—she drew herself up with a little wriggle, at the same time straightening the knives and forks on each side of her plate and looking from one to another of us with sudden matronly pleasure:

'Well, I think this very nice,' she said. 'It's very nice for me to meet Harry's best friend.'

A click of silence. Then Harry jumped quickly in, laughing:

'Steady the buffs, old thing! No wild heroics, you'll have us singing Rock of Ages—'

But she persisted:

'No, you mustn't laugh. I mean it. It means a lot to me, meeting Harry's best friend. Think of it,' she turned to where I was sitting, '*you* know all about Harry, and here's me knows next to nothing! I don't call it fair! Sti-ill . . . it's very nice, isn't it?'

Harry was as much startled by that 'best friend' as I was. It was plain she had misconstrued something he had said to her about me: perhaps 'oldest friend' —which was correct. Nevertheless it is very difficult, whatever the inaccuracy, to state openly that one is *not* a 'best friend.' It was an uneasy moment. At least she had lessened the blow by bringing in herself and the idea of my knowing much about his past life, which was of course quite true. And to this last point our minds and conversation quickly turned.

But for me the turn of her phrase was not so comforting—for as she said again that it was 'very nice' she had literally turned to me and had looked me straight in

the eyes. And in hers the dark-lashed there sparkled
a startling strength of meaning. She glittered at me,
a glitter old as sin, the wise old glitter that forces an
understanding between eyes, that burns down the
curtains of convention, that says: 'Look in, I'm not
only a name but I'm a person too. I'm not the terrible
apart. I'm a me—and I think I see clearly beyond
your defences that you may be you.' Something like
that. A glitter of liaison, a glitter deadset on collusion.

Earlier that lunchtime I had noticed, at times when
I was speaking particularly with Harry, how her eyes
seemed sometimes fixed on me. With careful study.
With interest. When I suddenly turned to her those eyes
dropped—with too much control she flicked ash onto
the carpet. At such times it is easy to be hopeful—or
simply vain. Knowing this too well, I had instantly
controlled the little rising worm and put down her
interest as the natural summing up of an intimate of
Harry's. But this last look was indisputable. I was not
being summed up, I was being invited.

I remember thinking: 'So. Another. Another sweet
predatory.' I was filled with pleasure and in the same
moment shocked at such disloyalty to Harry. But in a
second it was all over, and we had moved easily on to
talking of the old days. Harry described how we had
been at two schools together, I talked of our first days
in London, and Harry told me not for goodness' sake
to say too much.

'You'll get me blackballed,' he laughed.

Eve laughed too. And then, although we were a
dozen years older than she, rose easily from her twenty-
six or seven to looking back on her own twenties from
our same eminence. She began to tell us of her eighteenth

15

year, when she had spent several weeks in Budapest. I remember her rambling on:

'It was all just what you'd expect. All those uniforms, lovely iron pergolas in the restaurant gardens, tzigane music just everywhere you went, and a hussar band that played in the Zoological gardens—and oh, altogether you felt so much you were in the past, it may have been a silly past, but it *was* romantic. Of course there was the ordinary modern life too, you saw it everywhere—I remember a particularly horrid neon cross set on top of the oldest church in the city. But besides the romance you got roast goose and wine for breakfast in an ordinary cheap restaurant. We had that one night after a ball . . . yes . . . I remember that well . . .'

She paused then at some mysterious memory. She paused too heavily indeed for our comfort and particularly for Harry's, a sense of absence about her grew for a moment profound—then quickly she caught herself up and went on about her travels. Although what she said was on the whole very ordinary, a strong sincerity in her tone made it interesting and raised it above the naïve: and I was later to learn how often she talked of such things, of her past and of her small travels. It was part of her nature to find for herself purely and uncynically the romance in situations that have for many become unendurably hackneyed, spoiled by bad artists or kitsched by politics.

She went on, Harry was delighted to listen, and I was only too glad to be able to withdraw a little. I nodded and ah-ed and concentrated on thinking of something else—a double exercise useful at dull dinners. It is no good merely pretending to listen: one must also find an alternative subject and talk to oneself about this—hard. That afternoon I remember thinking of the sensory pleasures to be found—beyond all the old pro- and anti-functional arguments—in the sort of modern flats in which we were sitting. For instance, I said to myself—that pleasing sense of insulation, but with people near. And doors that close exactly on fitted carpet, that seal one up safe in a space not too large. Pleasures of shining appliances on their fat electric cords, the satisfaction of walls that make no sharp angle with the floor but at the very last moment curve into it and so subtly become it. Shadows cast with no nostalgic tree-patterns, but straight from sky to window, pale shadows as brightly mysterious as the grey ghost that follows one everywhere in the long nights of a polar summer. And a high overlook of trees, the rare consideration of trees from above, well-loved by the mandarin sage on his ladder of steps. And so on.

From time to time I took the precaution of returning —and found that while I had been to Lapland and Peking, Eve had been travelling up the Danube to Vienna. A dreary stretch of water, she was saying, a slow long chug against the mud-grey current and the land flat and dull to either side. It was fun to see Jugoslav and Hungarian captains spit at each other as their boats passed. And the variety of official cloaks at each landing-stage toned up the romance. And then Vienna —but ah, that was different!

A kind of holy look—and a real one, no affected spasm—came over her face. It was plain we were going to spend inspired minutes on the Ring, in and out of Sacher's we would go, and perhaps encoach for Schönbrunn. I adopted a second and rather more personal exercise of withdrawal. This is only polite when one is quite sure the speaker is high away in his speech. It consists again of agreeable nods, approving 'ah's'—a light rhythm designed to simulate the hypnosis the speaker intends but which in fact hypnotizes the speaker himself. This established, the second part of the exercise is to consider the speaker objectively in every aspect, from top to toe. It is not a nice exercise, it tends to be destructive.

What really, one says, what *really* is this in front of me? Thus I searched the impact of Eve's glamour. She was found to have two buttons missing from a formation on the right-hand cuff of her suit. Prickles of shaved fair hair came frosting through her stockings. There was the faintest fall of dandruff at her collar. She had a pale and flourishing but not unattractive moustache. The strength and surge of her breasts seemed sure— but nowadays one cannot be certain. Eyes lively and strange—of a pale colour, I still do not know what, encircled by dark lashes. I could not tell whether these were mascaraed or not, I think probably not. What she wore was, divested of herself, unparticular. She gave an impression of being 'dressed up'—but in fact she wore a most ordinary black suit of unexceptional cut and not too good a material. Her ornament was un-inspired, her shoes good. Her lips looked like any other lipsticked lips. But her hair—that indeed was excep-tional! It was brushed to a fine smooth lustre—it had the fine soft pewterish quality of sodium, camembert of metals. (You will have come across sodium. Take a brownish nugget, take a knife and cut through it easily and cleanly as fine cheese. There under the thin brown skin lies a soft smooth creamy metal like warm

pewter—unbelievably smooth, wonderfully soft! It is
not edible: throw your nugget into a bowl of water
and it catches fire.)

Eve was taking a light Riesling among the ferns and
plush of the Erzherzog Karl—and I was just wondering
what happened when she washed such an inflammable
growth, seeing that there was indeed an element of
fire latent in the lovely, pale-burnished, damp-dry
sheen . . . when the doorbell buzzed. Harry went out
and Eve stopped talking, Harry poked his head back
to say that it was the porter about his power fuses
and would we excuse him a minute?

A second later Eve turned to me and said in a low
abrupt voice:

'Tell me, do you think I ought to marry Harry?'

I must almost have jerked back as tensely her face
came forward. It was of course a well-known question.
At the best I never know the answer—but this from
Eve was a shock, and it took me a few seconds to see
the old question in its banal light and speak. One suspects that no more is wanted than an echo of confirma-
tion: though perhaps a certain doubt would be better
expressed, a doubt against which the inquisitor can
find arguments and thus further convince herself: at
the best, talk on the matter is what is most needed.
But just as at last I opened my mouth she went on
impatiently:

'Come on, you're his best friend. You're the only one
I can talk to about it.'

'But Miss—but Eve, Harry and I don't really see a lot
of each other. Not these days. It'd be truer to say,
perhaps, that I'm his oldest friend.'

'Well, old friends are best friends, aren't they?'

'I suppose, if you put it—'

'Well then, there you are! You're his best friend. Now don't hedge any more and tell me what you think.'

'But Eve, I'm sure you must be convinced—'

'No. Look here—will you do me a favour?'

Harry's voice was muffled in the hall. The porter's came clearly, a didactic thumb-in-waistcoat voice condescending to attentive Harry:

'. . . I meant t'say, you got your boxes of mains, hav'n't you? Right, you got your boxes of mains. See what I mean? . . .'

And Eve still whispered fierce, glancing round to the door, fixing me with meaning intimate glitter. She repeated:

'A *great* favour?'

'Of course. Anything you like. Anything.'

'Well . . .'

She paused. Took a breath. Then spurted:

'Let me come and see you.'

I must have looked dismayed. But she went quickly on:

'We haven't time to talk now. I must see you. Please —Harry's at the office all day, I could come one afternoon, could I? Could I ring you?'

'Eve, for heaven's sake! This is asking it a bit—it's conspiracy!'

'Well, whatever it is—quick—may I, may I ring you? When?'

'I don't know . . . it's . . .'

'May I?'

At last, but no longer wholly against my will, I nodded.

Her lips licked slowly back into a big appreciative smile—she sighed like one who has had a good meal. Then she half-closed her eyes at me, and raised a finger and gave a little tap in the air:

'Good. Then I'll ring. Early next week.'

The next instant she raised her voice:

'Harry! What on earth are you doing?'

'Coming!'

And in another second Harry came back and we carried on the rest of our luncheon outwardly as before. The same pale light came through the wide glass windows, the fawns and creams of the flat's furnishing sat clean and softly comforting, the musing modern mirrors meditated their afternoon calm undisturbed. Our cigarette smoke blued the air and soon a smell of coffee and cigars blended with the black perfume and the red lipline of Eve's presence.

But inside me, at least, there was no ease. Whatever Harry said seemed now to be answerable only with a lie. 'Eve and I thought of getting a little place in the country, not too far out!' Indeed! Or 'You don't know *Eve*'—and I was sitting there knowing I knew her. I could no longer feel honestly bored, no more sit back with the peculiar ease, undemanding and inexhaustible, one feels in dull company one rather likes. Instead I felt darkly excited, unpleasantly guilty. And that guilt as usual provoked its defence—attack: and I began to feel irritated that Harry was there at all. He was in the way. Intolerable of him.

But Eve showed no tremor of difference. She talked on equably, I felt even with greater energy, as if instead of shame she derived from this situation added power.

I made my excuses as soon as fairly I could. Out into

21

the bright March day, out from the dead smell of new flats. White clouds blew fast across a high blue sky. The newly gummy buds sparkled in such a fresh wind. A few early blossoms scattered pink on the grey pavements. Puddles caught the blue of the sky. I went home and tried, unsuccessfully, to work.

III

EVE telephoned early on Monday morning. She sounded very near, she had an intimate presenceful telephone voice:

'It's Eve, it's me.'

I was tempted to say 'Eve who?' I am always irritated by people announcing only their first names, openly announcing such consideration for themselves. It is even more irritating when one cannot help recognizing such a voice and cannot complain. I knew it was Eve, and so:

'Hello. How are you?'

'Remember what you promised?'

'Er—'

'Well, when?'

The day before I had been able to take a saner, fairer view of this predicament. Quite easily I had made up my mind not to see her. I had even been able to smile at the pathetic tricks of my simple double-faced emotions. Does one never grow wise, I thought? Looking back at myself as at some naughty little doggy, I had shaken my head in patient, amused reproof.

But now here was her voice in my ear, and its directness understood no refusal. My resolution slipped headlong:

'Then could you come in for a drink tonight—after five?'

'Why yes I'd love to. About five? Quarter past?'

'At a quarter past five.'

23

I replaced the receiver and cursed. But again, of course, the dark excitement had begun to bubble its light somewhere inside me—a bobbing of lanterns in the disapproving dark. Well, came the final shrug. As well today as any other time. What had to be had to be. It would have been impossible to put her off.

But in this, of course, I was wrong. One can put off people with endless facility. It is part of most people's, and particularly of a writer's, stock in trade. There are a dozen excuses, they can be used in rotation, and if these fail there are a dozen more. And certainly it would have been more graceful to have suggested a day later in the week—at least an outward grace of hesitation. And why did I suggest a drink, when the darkness was coming on—why not tea in the daylight? Whatever excuses I made to myself, the unconscious plan was evident. I even caught myself saying: 'If it comes to the worst, it's all for the best. Harry will be saved a worse awakening later.'

I can see I do not come at all well out of this. Later I was to come out, in a sense, worse. The least that can be said is that I made some pretence of fighting a losing battle. That is not much. And at least I did not resort to any of the reputable devices of the bachelor. No gramophone loaded with records of old Hawaii. No casual red cloth cast over the lights. No rearranging of cushions. No chance erotic poem left open. Certainly no incense. And none—as I have heard is happening these days—of those bottles of cheap hock in the kitchen ready for the sparklet and service by the glass as champagne. ('No messing about with bottles—straight, my lamb, to you from the fridge!') I took

24

none of these bachelor precautions. But then I nearly never do.

At a quarter to five I was already trying not to watch the clock. There was certainly half an hour more—and one should use half an hour, one should not treat one's flat as a railway platform.

But in one way my flat does in fact resemble a railway station—quite a large part of the main room is covered with glass. Once it was a drawing-room, latter-day Victorian, with a large conservatory attached. The conservatory has been kept in full working order, it is warm and full of plants, it smells of cemetery and jungle. Wide glass doors knicker out between the carpeted room and the mosaic floor beyond. Through these doors it is all ferns and big-leaved plants, and above them the curved glass cupola, ornamented with sinful magenta panes, that goes piering out over the garden.

At five o'clock—still much too early—I found myself setting out a tray of bottles and glasses on an abominable table of black wood inlaid with mother-of-pearl. When I took that flat, I asked a friend of mine with an eye for buying furniture to help me. 'Heaven!' he said, rolling his shoulders and beaming out at the conservatory. 'Purest Heaven! We'll make it plushy as tell your mum.' I told him that neither my mum nor her son would like that. I find it impossible to work in a heavily decorated room—especially in one heavy with marks of the past. However elegant an object of past period may be, that past always hangs about it, it carries a sense of something irretrievable and too strong to be endured. These beautiful things carry a malaise: in their company the mind cannot be free. I elected for a plain room, undistinguished, as bare as could be comfortable. I was served up with a compromise. So I turned my desk to those doors, and now work facing the fret and droop and flourish of such quiet green plants. But in this I fool myself, the conservatory has a date—somewhere about 1880—stamped all over it: and the plants in front are really every bit as distracting as the few furnitures behind. So that when my housekeeper at last showed Eve in, it was on a carved and whorled bean-shaped settee against those crinkling doors and the northern fust of plants that she came, graciously, to sit.

She had been hurrying. Her face was a little pink, her breath and her movements still agitated—as though for a time she must freewheel before running down. Nevertheless she took instantly to the appearance of the room.

'Oh,' she said, and her voice really meant it, 'it's beautiful.'

And most curiously, in the few seconds she took to realize the room, all the colour left her cheeks, her breathing subsided and she grew palely calm and absorbed. Again her strange eyes lost their presence and seemed to dream. With others such an abrupt transformation might have appeared affected: but not with Eve.

We went into the conservatory to look at the plants, to taste that green air. Eve wore the same black suit, but now her hair was covered by a small black hat with a furled veil at its shallow brim. It was warm under the glass, musty: the floorpipes dried the air and the thick green leaves seemed to moisten it, and against ferns like curtains of green bead, against young shoots curling out white, against darker fronds of heavy rubberplant and castor—Eve made a figure very alone, young, tragic, pale eyes kohled by unfulfilled dreams. She mixed instantly with the past.

I went in, and bending over the tray to mix our drinks I heard her footsteps faintly, thoughtfully, clicking the mosaic: then they ceased, and I knew she must be standing on the carpet behind me. I turned and gave her the drink. She sat down and as soon as that glass was in her hand the past faded, she sipped it and took out a cigarette, she perched herself cross-legged like any other girl of this age, and I am sure she felt it. How quickly those two moods had followed! An actress, I thought? But it was much more than that, it seemed less a capacity for absorbing her surroundings as an incapacity not to absorb and conform to them. It was not conscious, the rôles adopted her.

She was quieter than on the day we had met. She drank her drink very quickly, and put the glass on a side-table. When I asked her whether she would like another, she said 'yes' very quickly. I gave it her. I had no intention of making her drink a lot: but I saw no reason to object if she did.

Small talk with a writer or an artist is not so difficult as it is held to be—at least at first. There is his work to ask him about. It matters very little whether one has read it or not, it matters more to discover whether he writes on a typewriter or in longhand— that is a point which must early be ascertained. And see how uneasy and embarrassed he is! One is able to say of something: 'Of course, you know so much more about it than I do' (which one would never think to say to those equals, one's friends)—yet in five minutes venture more opinions on more matters than one has dared in months.

Just as a window-cleaner is used to terrified questions about the heights at which he must work—and the even more terrified tales of his questioner's experience at great heights—thus naturally the author-inquest is familiar. So it was pleasant to find that Eve did not bother with this. She seemed to prefer to talk about the room, and to me as perhaps a human being. Then, after her third drink, she took a decisive breath, settled herself more easily, and said in a quiet voice, suddenly intimate:

'I know you must think it odd of me to come here like this. But you see—I *had* to talk to you.'

I nodded gravely.

'Funnily enough I feel I *can* talk to you. You're one of the few people I feel I can talk to.'

She looked up and stared with her pale eyes straight into mine. Then she added, enunciating slowly the words:

'As woman to man.'

A heavy silence. I had been listening reverently but impatiently—both adoring her but impatient of these dismal gambits. Now suddenly I was out of my depth . . . what could that last mean? At all? Or was it meant only to sound like meaning? I fidgeted, and made a show of this, siphoning a drink both to break the silence and assure her, so that she would continue, that I was agitated.

'I want to tell you some things about myself, there are some things *you* ought to know. You know, I'm not quite the person Harry thinks I am. I think *you* might have guessed?'

She looked up at me sadly. Her pale eyes shone as if she were inwardly weeping. Her black lashes—mourning the grey? the blue?—suddenly reminded me of a widow's veil. And there was the veil on her hat. And behind her the green widowship of the past, sad ferns drooping their own green dusk.

'I don't know if you have guessed. You see, with you people—you're all so protected and sure. But my life's been different. I've had to fend for myself, I've come a long way. Of course the family were always well off, we had a nice place in the country—but I left. You know I ran away from home?'

I found myself nodding. Then changed this to a shake of the head. Of course I didn't know. But she made me feel I did.

'I ran away when I was seventeen. Seventeen. I'd know better now. Yet in a way I don't know—perhaps I'd do it again. I remember the day we left, raining, cold . . . beads on the carriage window, we wiped the steam off to look out . . . but that's not what I want to say. I must come to the point. It was later when I met —Erik—it's him I want to tell you about.'

She paused. And then went on speaking quickly, almost in defiance:

'We fell in love, Erik and I. Deeply in love. Silly name, Erik. We used to joke about it. . . . I even had to give it the "K", it sounded nobler! Now I know that was affected—but then we were younger, we had dreams and we saw life in a noble way even if it was silly. And we were in love—from the very first. He was —oh, whatever can one say—like a god? He was tall,

29

his strong teeth were always laughing. When he looked
at me . . . it was my first love, my only . . . we were
such kids, he was a student, I was working—we used
to go around with a gang of friends. Erik and Eve
they called us, the two Ees. Erik was a sort of leader,
it was he who inspired us, we did all the young, crazy,
careless things. They called me their mascot—they
were mad on their cars, fast cars open to the wind,
and they used to put me astride the bonnet when Erik
drove to a party and in that way we would come slowly
into the Mews . . . stupid . . . "the two Ees, easy does
it" they used to say—but it's easy to laugh now. We
never got engaged, Erik and I. We *were* engaged. It
didn't matter. We often talked of what we'd do when
we were married. When we had the money—and we
never doubted for a moment that the money, somehow
like a golden future, would be there. We were—dedi-
cated. We weren't lovers in the other sense. Erik re-
spected me. But how we—kissed! How we drove . . .!
Then one day he took up a plane. I saw my Erik up
high there in the blue sky, a little white bird—and then
he simply tottered, my love tottered. Something was
wrong. He was lame. It was soon all over. Dead. So
much so suddenly dead.'

Her young face was set with disgust, there were hard
lines from her nose to her lips, her lips sneered. I remember sitting there troubled and moved. Moved by
the old sad wedding, mythical and doomed beyond her
romantic storytelling, of young love and death: of lilac
and blood. And troubled by the scorn on her face, by
the filthy disillusionment of the young.

I went over and sat beside her. I murmured how
sad it was—and I meant it. But I took her hand—

and I meant that too. It rested, soft and strange, in mine: and she turned and looked miserably into my eyes. She looked away, and stubbed out a cigarette with her free hand. She had to lean away for the ash-tray—and thus the hand I held was the more mine.

'After that, well . . . I went to pieces. It was so unfair. Life seemed finished. There was nothing for me to do. The future disappeared. I went from job to job . . . and from man to man. I don't mean I . . . you know . . . I didn't do that, but I threw myself into a sort of vacuum of men, parties, all that emptiness . . . you know. I don't know why I'm telling you this, only I trust you. I've got to tell someone.'

I nodded and pressed her hand. She smiled again sadly—then suddenly her neck arched back and she said quite brightly:

'I'm not boring you?'

'Of course not.'

'Because if I'm boring you, you must just tell me. Just tell me and I'll stop.'

'Please—you're not at all.'

With her hand in mine I was not bored. But it was difficult about the drinks—how could I leave that hand and go over to the table? Would I get that hand back?

I went over to the table and poured gin. The sharp spirit smell rose and mixed with her perfume: with the dying day, these mixed smells excited. When I turned round with the glasses, she had taken her hat off and lit another cigarette.

'You don't mind me taking it off, do you? It's more homey. I *am* letting my hair down, aren't I?'

'Do make yourself at home. I'm glad.'

I was. Step by step we approach, I thought. I sat

31

down beside her again, a little nearer, and glanced down—my heart was beginning, there was repressive excitement in this formal approach when both of us were willing—for her hand. But now she held in one hand a glass and in the other her cigarette. I had forgotten about the glass.

'Not that I broke up completely,' she went on, 'I didn't do that. But it took the gilt off things. I never really got over it. It's not been easy since. I've never settled. It's been travel, and different jobs and different people. And I've got myself mixed up in things.'

She paused and looked at me sharply:

'Is that the right sort of girl for Harry?'

I took a drink, hoping she would follow. And vaguely said:

'Well . . . I don't quite see, what sort of things?'

'Oh . . . things.'

She looked round the room. She was searching herself for courage to begin. Then suddenly she blurted:

'Well there was Alec. I'd better tell you. I went away with Alec.'

Another pause, and then meaningfully:

'To the South of France.'

It was a question of either raising the eyebrows or keeping a very grave face. It was no time to take a drink.

But it would not have mattered, she was far away, and her voice grew soft as she stared out over the drink table to the conservatory:

'We went near to Toulon, to a little villa nearby. It was heaven, it was summer and pink oleanders grew all round the terrace where we worked. Alec was a sculptor. I was trying to draw. We stayed there until the leaves began to fall. I thought—really I was in love again. But then the inevitable happened.'

She stopped. I waited; but her mind evidently was filled with the picture of those times, and she brought up all we have so often heard—the purple sea streaked with turquoise, the blue hazed mountains behind, stone figures in the sun, the olives, the vine, the wine. It should have sounded very dull. But she was beautiful, and so sincerely away with her picture, so simply thrilled—it was quite pleasant to listen.

She had said, though, that about 'the inevitable'. It itched, and I had to interrupt her.

'Oh *that*,' she said. 'Well—just the old, old story. My dear sweet charming Alec had forgotten to tell me about his wife . . . who, conveniently, had been spending six months with her family in Canada. She had flown back rather suddenly, discovered Alec's address —and one day she just walked in.'

She shrugged her shoulders.

'And I just walked out.'

She frowned, and then set her chin.

'It was consuls, consuls all the way. I wasn't going to ask him for a penny. I slipped up to the room, packed a dress and things, and walked straight past them out of the door. They could think what they liked. And that was good-bye to Alec.'

I murmured approvingly. If she cared to tell me these things, she could—it was a method of bridging the first embarrassment, it was as good as any other method. Indeed it was better, for it demanded neither intellectual nor frivolous energies from me. I only had to wait. It was formal.

Moreover I had an adjustment to make. When Eve

had decided to visit me, I had at first resigned myself to the predicament. Then I had welcomed it. Then I had withdrawn a little into myself to regard her dispassionately the better to play the prelude to passion. But now—I found myself respecting her. I have said that beyond her banalities her evident sincerity charmed and convinced. Now I saw that in all her attitudes—stretching and crossing her long legs, lighting a cigarette carelessly, dreaming away beneath those heavy lashes, finding a green background to burn plushly behind her white profile—she was assured, complete, independent. Respect began to collide with strategy. The two were incompatible. It needed an adjustment, and a little time for this. Two things can be done at once, two moods felt: but it takes time.

However—it was six, past six. A definite move had to be made soon. I finished my drink quickly, intending to pour myself another while hers was still half-full: I was not prepared to compromise that hand with a further drink as yet. I was going over to the table—half-smiling at the sudden importance of this innocent 'holding hands'—when the telephone rang.

It was Harry.

Harry seldom telephoned. I have said we seldom met; similarly there was no reason to telephone. When I heard his voice, my voice must have sounded careful, I stressed his name.

'Why, *Harry*!'

Eve sat up.

Harry's voice sounded very near: 'That you, old man? Hope I'm not interrupting you?'

Eve began to wave her hands. She pointed to herself, she pencilled a finger up to her lips, she shook her head violently and a lock of her hair fell loose. Her mouth seemed to try to escape that up-pointed finger, it shook itself to and fro and the finger stayed still. All poise had dropped from her, she was a naughty small girl caught out, her eyebrows arched in appeal up, her whole body fluttered gawkish. She had dropped years.

Meanwhile Harry went on, less forbidding:

'. . . It's actually about a holiday, old man. Don't put off till tomorrow and all that—'

'I don't quite catch on, Harry.'

'Yes?'

'I said, what's that about tomorrow?'

'I don't know what you're talking about, old man. Sorry if I've disturbed you. But I've got to get this off my chest. Actually—I thought Eve and I ought to get away for a few weeks. Holiday. Spring. So I ran through my mind all the old places—where you and I've been. And I thought no, none of that, what's needed is somewhere fresh. Then I'd got you in mind, and I thought Eve likes to go abroad and I don't know much about that and there's you who do—so I said to myself, ring the old bastard. Now—what d'you suggest? Riviera? If so, where? What's good?'

'Well, Harry . . . I see what you mean . . .'

'Somewhere not too big, but a bit of life for the evenings. Good bathing. A touch of romance—know what I mean?'

I had thought Harry might be making some excuse to telephone, somehow he might have heard Eve was with me—but his tone of voice and what he said reassured me. In the old days Harry and I had very often spent our summer holidays together. We had gone regularly to the Channel coast. And Harry would not have been one to change much, he would have continued to go to those same places year after year long after those days. He did not know the rivieras, I knew them well: so it was quite natural he should telephone me.

But it was natural too that just then I should want to get him off the line. With Eve staring at the phone, eyes wide as a gambler's, it was not very pleasant to be speaking with him.

So I said quickly something like:

'I see exactly what you mean. But Harry, you've caught me at a difficult moment—I can't talk now. I couldn't say straight off, it's a thing needs speaking about at length. Can I ring you tomorrow? Will you be in the office?'

'Grand! Any time. And thanks awfully—this'll be a great surprise for Eve. I'm going to spring it on her, you know. Big surprise!'

'Good idea! Well . . . 'bye for now.'

'Cheeroh, old man.'

When I put down the receiver Eve gave a great outblowing sigh. She blew her cheeks and let out a whole air of escape:

'Heavens! Thank heavens that's over! What did he want?'

'What?'

'He didn't know I was here?'

'No.'

'Well what was it?'

'Oh, nothing.'

'Come on.'

'Mm . . . as a matter of fact, as a matter of—if you must know the old devil simply rang up to ask how I liked you, and didn't I think you were great, you know . . .'

'How sweet!'

'Yes.'

She mused smiling away at the floor, then suddenly looked up:

'I must say you didn't say much.'

'In the circumstances it was a little difficult.'

'So I need speaking about at length, do I?'

'At *very* great length. . . .'

'Well, now what *do* you think?'

She was laughing, mischief lighting up her face. No absence now, she was very near. Face shining, eyes of collusion.

One might have thought that Harry's voice would make me regret my position. It was the opposite. At first guilt had brought his voice too near. Then it had sounded very far away: safe, and as a third person most excluded. And Eve had made those motions of silence— again conspiracy, Eve and I against Harry. Another step together. And by now the few drinks had warmed the diffidence out of me.

She was smiling up delightedly as I went over. I sat down now right beside her, put my arm round her shoulder, so that our faces were close when I began:

'What do I think of you, Eve? That's going to be a long story indeed—'

But as I began, and as my arm slipped from the bone of friendship at her shoulder to the warmth of her waist, Eve did a very strange thing. Calmly, saying nothing and expressing on her face no change of emotion, so exceedingly at ease that even the ease did not need to be expressed, she disengaged herself from my arm. With no pose of averting herself, with neither coldness not archness nor reproof, she simply removed herself from me as if I had been a coat too warm. She did not even move away.

I stopped what I was saying. And then a terrible thing happened.

Puzzled and at a loss, I was watching her face. Her eyes were away, I was watching her mouth—when slowly, searchingly, the lips opened. They opened wavering in profile—I was so near I saw them silhouetted against the darkness behind, pink soft-painted lips each extended and wavering in the air as a separate organism, two pink-fleshed arms extended to receive fruit. But they were searching for a word—and then that word came down from her brain.

'Now we *must* talk about Harry. I must find out what you think about it, about us . . .'

She went on. I sank back away from her. I took a long drink. 'Bless her,' I thought, 'blast her. *She's simply come here to talk.*'

And so it was.

While I sat there feeling a fool, feeling at first angry, and then foolish, and then guilty—for failure increases guilt—and then a little later amused at the whole thing . . . while I sat there descending that hierarchy of emotions, Eve talked as she had intended to talk. I nodded, and altogether now at her disposal made whatever answers she intended I should make. For this was fireside oratory, she wanted simply to say to someone what had bubbled unspoken in her mind. She wanted someone to see her saying it, she wanted no criticism, no amendment. And she wanted—perhaps above all—conspiracy. Incredulous eyes! Whispered wonder! Nods, shakes, grunts, ahs, ohs, considerative mms. What she said had been said a thousand times before. But the imperative, wonderful point for her was that it was *she* who was saying it. One is tempted, in circumstances such as these, to call a halt, to stop the fuss and signify that such experience is not unique. But that is loose thinking. All experience is unique. It is only similar to other experience. It is happening to one person, perhaps for the first time, with the virgin wonder that goes with all first experience. If one denies this—the difference between what is similar and what is not unique—one might as well write off once and for all the individual.

Thus, devoted to the idea of the individual and just endurably weary of its exposition—thus I heard how in Eve's opinion marriage was a serious step. Many people today take that step knowing that there is always the escape of divorce—but not *she*. She understood by marriage a holy thing. Not that she was religious—that is, not ordinarily very. Besides, she wanted to settle. After the life she'd had. She'd told me a bit about that, but not by a long shot was it all. What she wanted to know was, should she tell Harry? No? But that wouldn't be trusting, that would be beginning wrong, people were broader-minded these days and besides her life had been unhappy, Harry would understand, he'd see how fate had started her off on the wrong foot—shouldn't she put her cards on the table, say take me, this is who I am? Yes? But that might be a shock, not that her life had been so shocking, not as all that—nevertheless Harry was such a sweet old dear, he was in a way so proper almost, he was the dependable type, and wouldn't it come as a shock? Perhaps it would be best to hint a bit, to test him out with a little to begin with? Only for his sake, of course. That would be better?

She told me about her home, her mother a silver-haired lady in grey lace, and embroidered this with a silver tea-set in the firelight. It was an ordinary, touching, but much spoiled scene of a small country home. Eve spoke of it with great longing. She invested every platitude with personal grace.

Then she was away again, easily drifting with the momentum of her mouth to Edinburgh. The Scots—how odd to find so methodical a people, such bridge-builders and material know-alls, with so brilliant a genius for dressing themselves up! What a fancy lot they were!

And there, I thought, she goes again—suddenly peppering her ring of platitudes with an idea not so usual. But it was all said on the same level. The unkind thought had to suggest itself—men. She was simply repeating a series of opinions instilled into her by a series of men she had known. This may too easily happen. Women retain knowledge like the layers in serpentine rock. Men marshal it into a definite, if un-balanced, whole. Strata of women, conglomerate of men.

Anyhow, if it was men, it had nothing to do with me. It was plain I was not to figure among those chosen. Unless as a mixture of confessor uncle and conspirator. Thus I sat on and gave her her head. The dissimilarity between our ages began to grow plain and huge, the space between us echoed like a wide long light. I felt an elderly, stupid, a dear old impotent husk.

After she had at length left, I went to my cellar and brought out a wine of unusual excellence. A treat, a resurrection of self-respect.

IV

BUT she persisted. In my mind. And it may have been this that made me take an unpredicted step when I telephoned Harry the next morning.

It was a wet day, I was up and bathed and dressed by something after ten, and I remember watching the March sky through the window. The rain dribbled from a well-laundered cloud-cloth. Occasional gusts of ragged brown blew slowly across. Yet it was warm, moist. Bright dull weather of childhood Monday mornings; when a smell of washing hangs damp and one is left, without sunshine and in neutral light, outcast of copper and clothesline, alone. Everyone else too busy to play. Weather for washing—and now in adult age weather for the travel agency and dreams of an orange south.

It may have been such empty weather that started a sort of tolling in my mind. An imprecision echoed: I found I was suspecting that Eve had wanted to say much more than she already had. Then I put this down to my own frustration. But whatever—it must have moved me to say what I did when I telephoned Harry.

His voice was brisk—then broadened out in his friendly way:

'Hello? Who? Oh—it's you, hello . . . this *is* quick work . . . you *are* a speedy individual—'

'Harry, I've been thinking. It's some time since I was down in France there—things might have changed —they're building a lot, opening the little places up.

41

I think the best for you would be to go somewhere solid and central like Nice and motor out a couple of days. You've got the car? I could suggest a few points to aim at.'

'Good idea. Nice all right? For a start?'

'Very pleasant—don't believe what people tell you.'

'People . . .? Don't see . . .? Heavens, I wish you were coming down with us. . . .'

It was then that I found myself saying, carefully, as if I were hearing someone else's words:

'Why not? Why . . . not?'

Harry's voice spluttered distantly:

'No! . . . You would?'

By then I had begun to wonder why I had said that.

'No, Harry. You mustn't take me seriously. . . .'

'But you *were* serious. I know that voice.'

'I wouldn't think of it. With you and Eve! Three's no company.'

Harry put on a firm games-master voice:

'Hell, it'd be like old times. I'm not going to let you get out of this. . . .'

Nor did he.

Five minutes later I had agreed to go across with them in three weeks' time. We would drive in Harry's car. He would see to the tickets—I was to work out where we should stop on the way down. And in those five minutes I felt indeed an enthusiasm rise for the project. By then I had already rationalized my behaviour. In the first place it was time to go south, March willed it. And it was good theory to travel not with a close friend but with some sort of disinterested acquaintance. Close friends take too much of the passing scene themselves: tastes and wishes must be

42

considered: it is not always easy to excuse oneself into solitude: and always, always just as one notices something and wants to digest it—so there comes a tug on the arm and a friendly voice points out something else: 'But look *there*, but look at *that*.' Better even to travel with an enemy—loneliness is averted and solitude secured. Yet the best of all travelling companions is a couple still interested in each other. They can be escaped from: they are available a little. And if one is open to the possibilities of a romance— and who in season is not?—the woman is useful, she decoys other women. A lonely man is left alone, a man in a party with a woman becomes a target.

So I thought this was fine, and it was fixed. Then Harry said:

'Capital! Now—when'll we meet? Soon as possible, eh?'

'Meet?'

'To discuss it.'

'But we've already discussed it.'

'Nonsense, we've got to talk this kind of thing over.'

We had spent ten minutes discussing it, everything was arranged, there was no more to say. But there— Harry was excited, so I thought the best thing might be to get it over:

'Would you be free this afternoon? I'll be near your office.'

'In the office? Good-oh! Anytime after five.'

And so late that afternoon I walked from Chelsea through the tatterings of Pimlico to Victoria Street. There, lurking behind Whitehall, stood the red-stone offices where Harry contracted his marine brasses. All up the façade pottery wreathed in hard florescence:

but the years had drabbed it all, pottery and brick, with grit and grey soot. Inside a similar gloom prevailed. Tiles grimed the walls, fawn-coloured wood dadoed a bare stone stairway. But a smart blue attendant drove me up in a heavy steel lift—for this was engineers' ground—and soon I was knocking on the frost-panelled door of Harry's office.

I poked my head round the door. Poking the head round office doors—only the head—is exhilarating: one thrills at the same time with reticence and a maximum intrusion.

Harry flung a hand out, gripping with the other some papers:

'On the dot! Take a pew. . . . And look who's here!'

Eve was making idle arcs of herself in a swivelling chair. As women do in male offices, she looked masterful and erotic.

'Well, of all the—I thought this was a surprise, Harry?'

'Shh!'

Eve picked up with her slender red fingernails a T-square, her nails slid about the brown wood like lacquered weevils. Swivelling she pointed at us:

'What surprise? What *is* all this?'

Harry pressed his lips together, frowned, and leaned forcefully forward over the desk, saying in a severe voice:

'It's just this, my girl . . .'

She raised her eyebrows. He gave a great smiling thump on the desk:

'. . . that our friend here and myself are taking you off to the South of France for a holiday!'

Her eyes opened wide. Her face fell and she looked

44

for a second frightened. Then she caught herself, smiled, made an unbelieving look, looked all over the room for a means of speech. She stopped swivelling. At length:

'B . . . but . . . I don't know what to say! It's wonderful!'

'I thought that'd bowl you.'

'Harry—but when?'

'In precisely three weeks' time!'

It was plain she was frightened. Harry never noticed, he went straight on explaining how we were going and where and when. He got up from the desk and walked over to the wide old sash window, he talked on through this to the well of grimed white tiles outside. He talked of mimosa, and light from the tiles greyed his hair and picked out fragments of fluff on his dark blue suit. Slowly Eve began to swing again on her chair: but now there was no doubt of a tension in her, she was acting unconcern.

It was infectious, I grew nervous, I was mystified. But why? I stared at a framed photograph of a Japanese cruiser and wondered. It crossed my mind she might think this was a trick of Harry's to get her away with him, to preamble the marriage-bed. But to see him standing there among his long rolls of blue-print by his hatstand with its bowler and its clothesbrush, on the quiet turkey carpet and in that austere light of curtainless window whose blind-cords hung so still— it seemed absurd. Besides—I had no idea whether they had not gone to bed together already. I knew Harry was normally sensual. But he was, in compartments, strictly conventional. It would appear to him logical to seduce someone else's sister and half murder the man who seduced his own. Now, having proposed marriage, I had an idea he would honour and respect the idea of marriage. It was in his nature. And it was inevitable that Eve's instinct should tell her this.

Then what?

My thought returned naturally to the man she had told me about—but that had been long ago, they had taken the villa temporarily, there would surely be no fear of his remaining there? No.

But it was extraordinary how she had collapsed. She sat now hemmed in by the office, by bookcased directories and the pale unvarnished wood. And suddenly Harry saw this too, he turned from what he was saying and saw how she sat swivelling ill-at-ease:

'Darling—*you* don't seem too bucked!'

She looked up brightly:

'Me?'

'Yes, you! Why so dubious? Where's the funeral? This is an occasion for merriment.'

She laughed. Then said soberly:

'It's just so sudden. I was thinking—'

He looked concerned, his voice came apologetic:

'How stupid of me—I'd forgotten you know the place yourself. It's not so special for you—but I just thought you'd like it, you've *said* you like it. . . .'

She looked quickly sideways. Then firmly:

'But I *haven't* been there. It's not that, no . . .'

'Not been?'

'Never the riviera.'

'But you told me—I thought—isn't Cap Martin somewhere there?'

'Cap Martin?'

'Yes, you said about a holiday once . . .'

46

'Oh—'

She paused a moment. Then:

'You've mixed it. It's the Italian riviera I went to. Cap Martin—I know, it must have been Margherita ... Martin—Margherita. Santa Margherita near Genoa. It's different. . . .'

'Funny. I could have sworn—'

'No. But this'll be new.'

'Eve—you are keen to go?'

She lifted her feet off the ground and spun herself once completely round. As she slowed to a stop she sighed out a sort of giggle:

'See. No handlebars.'

Harry smiled and went on about the Route Nationale —was it the best way? Or what about the Alps—it might be fun to cross through the cold?

For some extraordinary reason it had been worth her while telling Harry at length about Cap Martin and calling it Toulon to me. Then openly, obviously denying them both. She felt perhaps powerful enough to confuse Harry—and possibly trustful enough of me to keep quiet. But why the lie? There could only be that old love affair at the bottom of it—she simply did not want to revisit the atmosphere of that distant affair. She had been too happy.

I began to fear for Harry again. And more and more to dislike my own rôle of confidant.

Eve suddenly broke in:

'But Harry, what about my job? What about that contract?'

'Contract? I thought you just worked from day to day?'

'Well there's no contract really . . .'

'Then there's nothing to get out of. They'll get someone else easily enough.'

'Thank you.'

'I didn't mean that.'

'It's nice to know one can be as easily replaced as that.'

'Darling, you know what I mean. They *can* get someone or other.'

'Don't be too sure.'

I saw Harry's forehead crease with sympathy, his hand fall defenceless to his side. He measured the air with seriousness. He was all humility, all sympathy—he was at his strongest.

'Eve, I *do* see what you mean.'

'You don't.'

'And *I* know you're hiding something.'

Eve looked up. He went on:

'I don't think I'd be far wrong if I said you were really just sorry to let them down.'

'What?'

'You want to play fair, and you're damned right. You are, really.'

'W-well . . .'

'But what you forget, Eve, is that they're a big firm. This sort of thing often happens to them. They're organized. They'll have alternatives ready—they couldn't afford to risk not.'

'But I said . . .'

'Now don't you worry your head about it any longer. Look, phone them tomorrow. Or if you like I'll do it. Don't-you-worry-your-head-about-it. . . .'

This humbly reasonable Harry usually won. It was his most loveless trait. Perhaps he was not to blame—

48

it was part of the legacy of a salesman's life. His line was binnacles and propellers—he was in fact an ex-engineer travelling in ship's equipment—and with such matters he had no need to push and boast. But there he was in greater danger, for he had to talk with reason to intelligent men—he had to distort both intelligence and reason. And Harry was honest. So he had to believe in his distortions. And so he lived them. And carried them into his private life.

Honest but shrewd too—for now instantly he proposed a drink, gone was the need for discussion, he was making sure of a sort of wave to carry us all along.

And we were willing, Eve was glad of a respite, I was only too glad to be away from that Japanese cruiser. That cruiser sailing the dark brown sea of its photograph brought to mind occasions of naval review, it spoke of the plucky little Jap monkeys grinning all over their huge ship at Spithead before 1914 and of the yellow swine encountered in the Pacific in 1945. It spoke to me of the deception of wars. That mighty and beautiful ship of battle could speak now only of deception—and while we talked it echoed the subtle deceptive atmosphere that day in Harry's office.

We took a taxi, and the dark leather box—always good for a moment's exhilaration—brought relief to our slight, unspoken restraint. When Eve had settled in, and long after the taxi had started off, Harry and I were still offering each other the comfortable back-seat beside Eve, standing crouched, flipping up and down the small front seats. This made for grunting and giggles. But when Harry with his head on the roof began to declaim: 'Après vous, Monsieur!' I thought that was enough, we didn't want to start *that* one, and I sat down. And of course Eve then carolled: 'But there's plenty of room, plenty for all,' and Harry lurched down beside her. There was not room, she in the middle had to sit on the edge upright.

We were going to some club of Eve's. All the way there she proudly ran it down. 'Not much of a place. Just somewhere to slip in.' The warmth of her legs crept through to mine, her perfume came strong as her voice now so near: I had intended to excuse myself —we were on my way home—but now I thought, 'a little longer'. And so, talking now of everything else but our expedition south, we joggled along into Belgravia. The streetlamps were lit, it was a damp misted night. The lonely lamps, dripping façades, dark shapes of trees, smelled of a London long ago.

Eve's club had a striped blind on its pillared porch, we went in and signed our names by a trellis of white wrought iron. That iron was wood, the cream walls were rough-cast plaster, and white plaster frames encircled so many mirrors that one was always catching sight of that uneasy stranger, oneself. Gold-painted candlesticks, renaissance chairs of fringed silk, draped green curtains and heaven knows what else gave this elaborate mushroom the air of a shop-window display. At any moment the plaster might crumble, at a sign the colours would change to yellow and brown and the carpet would grow a scattering of autumnal gloves, a riding crop, a stylized terrier. Over the bar a striped awning gave a touch of Paris-sur-Gore—and to this we went, avoiding chairs fashioned more for the eye than the seasoned rump.

Eve swept ahead, nodded to two people standing by

a white midget piano, and drew the barman from his evening paper:

'Sho-op!'

Again she assumed easily a new atmosphere. A brittle new vivacity swung her up on a stool, patted her hair in the mirror, and enlivened her to a mock play of secrecy with the note that Harry now began to stutter at her beneath the bar.

'I'm the member, you know!' she said.

Then she turned to us. 'It's not Harry's sort of place really, is it? He's more at home in one of those great dreary men's clubs.'

'But I like it here,' Harry said. 'It's bright. It's Bohemian.'

It looked very dull. Only two other people in the room with us, and they talked softly, they sighed between silences like ladies tired in a tea-shop. Eve said:

'It brightens up later—you should see them at closing time!'

Then she was turning round to the two at the end of the counter—not two ladies but one ample gentleman in an overcoat, his black businessman's trilby still in his hand; the other a grey-haired lady in tweeds, frail but erect, her face scrubbed so clean that for a while it was unnoticeable.

'Hello you two, Barney! Martie! . . . where's the funeral?'

'It's a cremation, dear,' the fat man wheezed back quick. 'Cremation on account of this blisterin ot weather.'

'What'll you have to cool you? A bucket of ice?'

The man Barney made a third muscle of his chin

as he lowered his black-rimmed glasses down to what he held in his hand:

'Don't mind if I do dear.'

Eve laughed gaily, and rapped Harry's change at the barman. Suspicions began again to rise in me—could such brightness be true? Or was it to cover her anxiety? She smiled widely now at the tweeded woman, over-sweetly, woman-to-woman, and asked her what was hers?

Now these two came over, and Eve pushed the ice-bucket over to the fat man:

'Bucket of the weather for one, Mr. Barnett.'

He chuckled hoarse down in his big belly:

'Bucket of the weather eh? Bucket of the whether or not more likely—whether or not we'll survive at all this perishin cold more like.'

He looked at us over his big black-rimmed spectacles. He had weak pale blue eyes that looked kind. He went on hoarsely:

'Mows the old uns down like skittles. Time of the year. 3 ack emma, there's your hour! Cold in the bones, they can't stand it—ang your ead out the window and you ear em poppin off all down the street. Scotch thank you Tom.'

'Aren't you morbid!' Eve winced.

'Don't pay any attention to Barney,' came a surprisingly firm deep voice from the frail face of the lady with him. 'Plenty of them old uns'll see him under first, if you ask *me*. Why look at him, quivering with cold!' She suddenly laughed, and her eyes sparkled. I suddenly saw she had a big mole with a long hair on her chin: 'Quivering with cold! Or should I say *quavering*?'

Mr. Barnett looked at her with almost a coy look.

'Quavering? Any more from you and I'll get *crotchety*.'

This was a little above my head. Nobody could sound less crotchety than this Mr. Barnett. He had the face of a well-filled, hail-fellow commercial traveller. With his black trilby, his thick neck and his heavy-rimmed glasses he brought to mind early-morning beer in empty bars.

'Crotchets? Quavers? That's good!' Eve shouted. She turned to me:

'Mr. Barnett's a music publisher.'

Mr. Barnett shook hands and looked at me playfully over his spectacles. 'You bowl me over,' he said.

I stared hard into his glasses. I could not think. Drunk? Then the deeptoned lady started talking to the chair she had just left: 'Come to Martie, come on,' she cooed to the green leather. I found myself watching the chair hard.

Then it all came right—Mr. Barnett said: 'Title of my latest smash-hit.' And from underneath the chair crawled a long old sealyham.

Eve trilled: 'Oh the sweet, it's Audrey it is.'

Audrey shook her head violently, caught a shag of hair on her overhanging blue lip and sneezed.

'The sweet, she's got herself a cold!'

'Good dog,' said Harry hopefully, wanting to say something. And then forgetting his prudence, I suppose still wanting to talk, he gave a shiver:

'Jove, you're right about the weather. But we're cutting out, you know. The three of us going south for a bit of sun.'

Barnett looked startled: 'Brighton? Bit rough, aint it?'

'Well not exactly Brighton. We're . . .'

But it was Eve who now took a deep breath and gave an ecstatic account of what we three proposed. She explained our route, our destination: and added much which had never been discussed. My spirits fell. Such enthusiasm meant no good. Nobody could change so quickly. She had something up her sleeve.

'The mimosa will be out,' she cried. 'And think of the food!'

'Great juicy steaks!' growled Mr. Barnett.

'I can never understand,' a strange voice from behind me said, 'why any reference to the eyries of high cuisine sends my countrymen champing about steaks. Once it was to get away from steaks we went to France.'

A strange voice? Not so strange. I turned round to see someone I slightly knew—a Roddy Meredith, a dilettante in decor, in fact the same one who had made of my own house so uneasy a travesty. It was surprising to see him in such a place. Roddy's life was planned on more fastidious ground. Sometimes, when things were bad, it was: 'Meet me at the Ritz and we'll go across to the Express Dee.' But never, never did he venture in between.

Yet he seemed to be known—he nodded to the others. He looked Eve over quickly:

'Oh what a pretty brooch!' he said peering close at it—not at her.

I was interested to see that he knew her. When they had all started talking again, I got hold of him as he ordered a drink and whispered:

'What on earth brings *you* here?'

'And for that matter, same to *you*.'

I pointed to Eve and Harry: 'Old friends.'

He over-raised his eyebrows: 'What—*she*?'

He gave me a mischievous little flutter, then before I could ask him what he meant, went on about himself:

'Why am I here? I daren't tell you.' He dropped his voice and made a face of pain: 'I did it.'

'Did what?'

'This . . . all this . . . the beautiful mirrors, the sleazy bloody drapes. Torture.'

'Then why did you do it, Roddy?'

'Money.'

'But you can do better than this. . . .'

'They'd have turned it down. It's the old story. Call in the expert, shower him with shekels, feel a good boy because you've paid—then cut the expertise and tell him to do what *you* want. I just imagine what they want first and go ahead. Less bother.'

Over his shoulder I saw Eve still flashing on about the beauties of a French riviera she was supposed never to have visited. It sounded surprisingly accurate. Mr. Barnett had strolled over to the piano, and, one finger protruding from his mass of flesh and overcoat, now jabbed out single notes and muttered in a sudden soft tenor·

> 'You bowled me over
> In your own little body-line way.
> You took my wicket,
> It wasn't cricket,
> How can you say it's fair play . . .?'

And then as Roddy went on talking, a disturbing memory came to me. He was talking of his business in Georgian and early Victorian objets d'œil. He called it 'tat':

'It's *torment*. The country's been *combed*. All the pretty things have been bought and sold *twice* over. Me, know what I'm doing now? It's the *end.* . . .'

'No?'

'Potting castor-plants. In bloody pos.'

'Pose?'

'Under-the-beds. The amusing ones, roses and all get out. Bloody jerries—they're all that's left.'

I pretended to laugh while he described how half his clientele had to have the handles knocked off—but all the time his voice was recalling to me a scene some months back in Hyde Park. I had been strolling with Roddy. I did not know him well—but I always liked his frivolity, it was a relief. And in a bitter brittle way he had a good mind.

It had been a day of racing clouds and sudden bursts of sunshine. Into one of these, as into an apocalyptic bright light, there rode a detachment of Household Cavalry. Against the wintry trees their silver flash, their fine black horses and flowing blue topcoats made a brave show—their red plumes sang and their harness jingled bell-music in the clear air. It was very beautiful.

'The second one in the fourth row's *my* cup!'

Roddy made an act of simpering, taking off that sort of talk—though in fact he himself never managed much else. It didn't match the atmosphere, and I shut him up. But it was difficult to shut Roddy up, and soon he was chattering away again, starting up some story about somebody we knew, asking my opinion as to whether so-and-so should be kept apart from so-and-so, because so-and-so had left so-and-so. I suppose because I was moved by the vision of those cavalry still passing, I tried to shut him up again too abruptly:

'For God's sake, Roddy. How should I know? It's their own affair.'

His voice lost its ring of gossip:

'Well I was only asking. I just don't think they should meet again. I'd *stop* them meeting.'

'It's hardly your business. How can you know what's involved? Only those concerned can really know what they want.'

'One can form one's opinion. Surely one can have that?'

'Outside opinion, Roddy. You shouldn't presume to advise.'

'But put yourself in their situation!'

'Since I am not them, it would be foolish and inaccurate.'

I kept myself from saying that most of such advice was impelled by pure joy in a 'situation'. The cavalry were receding, they were bobbing far down the sandy Row, a group of brazen tulips still flashing in the sun —when Roddy stopped suddenly and said with real astonishment in his voice:

'But don't you want to *help* your friends?'

It was a simple phrase. It was unlikely that Roddy meant it altogether sincerely—but at that time, in the pause after those cavalry had passed, the simple words struck me with their full meaning.

I began to wonder. Was it after all not a duty to help in the affairs of others—even to intrude? Too much of this present cult of non-interference? Non-interference become indifference? And was I not in any case obsessed by my disgust with the lips of gossip, the heightened voice, the brightened eye—so that I avoided it all too easily?

C
57

That day in the park that question was brought, by a chance glitter of cavalry, home to me. And it was brought home to me again that evening in the plastery, bright-lit bar. I found myself certain that Eve was hiding something. And Harry suspected nothing. Harry Camberley was my old friend, there was that odd confusing bloodtie, there was no doubt I felt a kind of loyalty towards him. Eve was charming, I liked her—but she was dangerous.

Barnett was still being bowled over at his little piano:

> 'Adorable witch
> You queered my pitch,'

Then I heard Harry's voice, more at ease: 'Now Eve—less romancing. We've got to get down to brass tacks. Clothes to be got—that's your job. Tickets—that's mine, I'll get 'em tomorrow.'

Eve linked her arm in his, smoothed his hair. 'And who,' she purred, 'buys tickets for whose little own motorcar?'

He smiled: 'And whose little own motorcar takes the plunge into which little old channel?'

I thought then her face fell for a second. She frowned: 'Channel?' And then picked up: 'Of course, the boat tickets. Well since I'm going shopping, I'll be around. *I'll* get them. Leave that to *me*.'

She was talking too quickly. I felt she meant to forget to get them. I then interfered:

'No, Eve—let me get them. Harry's driving us—let me make some sort of contribution.'

'But I'll be passing . . .'

'No, I simply won't hear of it.'

It seemed so important to defeat her intention that

I forgot that I was in fact interfering in the wrong direction. It would have been wiser to let her go ahead and shipwreck the crossing. But I insisted. Eve gave me an uneasy look.

Then suddenly Roddy said: 'It never rains but it pours, does it now? I'm off too. . . .'

'Off?'

'South.'

'Then business can't be quite so bad. Where are you going?'

He stalled: 'Where are you?'

'Nice—to begin with.'

He made a sigh of mock relief: 'Arles,' he sighed.

That was to put a safety belt between us. And yet to be somehow somewhere near. In the same way Roddy would never accept an invitation. He made a half-excuse. He always said he *might* come; very often he arrived. For this reason I did not get Harry to offer him a lift. It would have meant too much double-talk.

We ordered more drinks. The woman Martie was talking—as she talked her well-washed neutral face became alive, that long hair from her mole wagged in the air with what seemed joy as her jaw moved. It turned out she was a breeder of dogs. Not so surprising —for with her tweeds and her efficiently bunned hair she looked indeed the very woman to breed a dog or bottle a pear. There was a sniff of the Downs about her. And in every feature of her face there were graven lines of kindness and sympathy: and firmness. Her eyes were grey and friendly—and they looked the clearer for heavy tufted eyebrows. In repose her face was just scrubbed flesh and hair: talking, it was the liveliest in

59

that room. And, of course, talking brought to light her only really strange feature — her deep uvular boom.

Now linking France with dogs, she was upbraiding the poodle.

'A lot of dressed up nonsense,' that voice said—it was not a hearty boom, it was slow and measured as a walk round the garden—'but it's not for me to grumble, I turn quite a pretty penny out of the fellows myself. Ever hear why they clipped them in the first place? Duck-shooting,' she boomed, 'in Russia.'

'No!'

'I can feel,' Roddy said, 'how the ducks felt.'

'The ducks didn't see them, you silly. It was for swimming. Just like these fellows—like Audrey—bred for ferreting. Bred long to get down holes.'

Roddy looked down at Audrey, who was staring hairily, at her level, at nothing at all. 'Hear that, Audrey? Proud girl?'

Audrey looked up mournfully, and then from somewhere deep in her shag trembled a high desolated pipe.

'Poor mite, she wants to go out,' Eve said. And then in afterthought: 'Diddums den?'

'Mite!' barked Martie. 'Audrey's eighty if she's a day.'

Roddy bent down to Audrey crooning compassion for her great age, fussing. He knelt down neatly, knees close together. A look of interest came to Audrey's eyes, somewhere far behind her a tired stump of tail tremored a wag. Here was attention, always pleasing! Attention for Roddy too—for now everyone looked down at the two—and Roddy prodigal of the fine crease of his trousers bent his head to Audrey, managing to make an elegant nursery group of himself and the bitch. He began to whisper confidences. Audrey, perhaps feeling that some service was required of her, swayed to her four feet. She exposed what had been hidden, a double row of fat tired dugs pink where the old hair had receded. It gave her a look of having six— or was it eight?—more feet: she looked like a snout-footed caterpillar.

Then Roddy put his head on the floor, and for perhaps the first time in her life Audrey found herself looking down on a human god. And she found she liked it. From her new great height she gave a brittle whimper of joy and stuck up one ragged ear—she had heard deep in her cankerous drum some ancient call of the wild. Roddy was equally moved, and between them they fuelled the fires of a minor hysteria down on the carpet by the bar-stool-legs. Soon Roddy was discarding words for a sing-song doggy whine. Audrey went down on her fore-paws and gave an imitation of a bark. Roddy made paws of his hands, and slapped one of Audrey's. Unluckily, he landed on a cyst. Audrey squealed and shuddered backwards; but instantly forgave, forgot, and bounded forward swinging her massive dugs in pink carillon. Roddy snapped. Audrey yelped. Roddy barked. Martie playfully kicked his behind. Audrey, her hair all down her eyes, panted into what looked like laughter. Then Roddy caught hold of her paws and began to dance out the words of a bog-fairy song popular then in the night-clubs:

> 'I'm Stinkabelle,
> Stinkabelle,
> Stinkabelle the Fairy!'

Audrey now laughed openly, a wild-horse look rolled white in one eye.

> 'I hold my court
> In a bladderwort
> (Oh it's perfectly sanit-ary:).'

Over by the piano the great black shape of Barnett, ostensibly singing nonchalantly for himself, raised his voice:

> 'Now, it's our dream
> To build our *own* team
> In the wonderful Bye and Bye.'

And Roddy yelled:

> 'King Oberon's Wand
> On me back o' beyond!
> I'm Stinkabelle the Fairy.'

Martie boomed, 'Go on, Audrey, dance dear!' Harry began to laugh, Eve began to bark, Audrey had got quite beyond herself laughing and yelping and not knowing what next or which end her tail was —altogether a slight pandemonium rose in that little smoke-hung corner of brightness in the bar.

It rose like a breath of circling wind, it whirred up to a small cyclone of sound and wits all blurred—and Roddy went too far. He pounced forward and kissed Audrey on her great blue lips. And Audrey's lips, quivering like the soft flesh of a lobster claw, sent a cry of panic to her brain. She kissed back—but with all her teeth. Roddy gave his greatest yelp, and blood streamed out over one eyebrow.

'Bitch!'

'She might have got your eye!'

'Bit 'is eye?'

'Damn . . . damn. . . .'

Roddy was still kneeling, a hand to his forehead, surprised and suddenly strained to see the blood on his fingers. Martie was looking for Audrey who had backed yelping under a stool:

'You over-excited her... Audrey, come to mama....'

But Eve was the only one who did anything. She was straight down on her knees with Roddy, wiping the blood away and looking for the size of the bite. At the same time she was speaking clearly above all the others to the barman: 'Thomas, a jug of water—quick!' And to Harry: 'Chemist over the road—iodine—and ask about dog-bites.'

She was instantly capable. And efficient. And sensible and calm with it. She had not hesitated to use her handkerchief and to kneel down laddering her stockings. And very patiently she wiped the wound. I saw in her then the greatest beauty of women—their great removed patience, as when for long calm hours they iron clothes, as when with absent eyes they suckle a child.

And for a long time—while the moment's panic subsided, while one by one they saw it was not so serious and until at last Harry came back with the iodine and the news that anything like hydrophobia was out of the question—all this time Eve was thus patiently absorbed. I watched her, and I was glad to see how she was so much of a woman. When it was over I found myself saying:

'It's all right, Eve. *You* can get the tickets.'

Of course, she didn't understand me. Nor did anyone else. There was an absurd silence. I bit my tongue—and then, thank God, old Mr. Barnett began to laugh, he thought I had made a joke he ought to understand. So he made sure of understanding it, he gurgled deep inside his overcoat. 'That's rich,' he laughed. Then he thumped loudly for drinks, shouting: 'That's the ticket!'

The matter was over, and in the little confusion of sorting out drinks I took the opportunity to make my goodbyes. The next morning I went out and bought those tickets.

V

BUT I need never have bothered. Two weeks later, three days before we were due to go, Harry telephoned to say it was all off:

'But there's no help for it,' he told me, 'Eve's got to go down to look after this Aunt of hers. Martie's driving her down tomorrow. God, can't tell you how sorry I am.'

'Well Harry—it just can't be helped, can it? Don't worry.'

'But it's put you out so. I·can't—'

'I'd have been working down there anyway. I can work equally well here. Forget it, please.'

'Oh—then you won't go?'

'W-ell . . . well at that I might. I don't know. I'll have to think.'

'I phoned you right away. I've only just heard myself. It's all a bit abrupt—why not come round?'

'If you like, yes. When? This evening?'

'Fine. About six. Again—most terribly sorry. . . .'

I hung up with mixed feelings—I hated the inconvenience, but I was shamefully pleased that I had been right about Eve. I never doubted that this sudden illness of her Aunt was an excuse. It was clever of her to have played along with us all this time—she must have intended it from the beginning, she must have lied her way through all her shopping, through all the excited plans that as fellow travellers we had since improvised. However, Harry seemed to believe her. His voice was genuinely apologetic.

Nevertheless, my plans had been upset—and now I found myself glad to go round and talk about them: this was the same fussiness to talk about things that I had deplored in Harry when he had asked me to his office two weeks before. Now I was only too happy to lose my sudden loss in talk.

But I was unprepared for the atmosphere that greeted me. At first he was surprised to see me: 'You didn't get my message?'

'No. I've been out.'

'Oh, I see.'

'What message? I hope nothing's—'

He kept his hand on the doorhandle, he seemed uncertain about letting me into the flat: then he recovered himself: 'Oh it was nothing.'

'But a message? Harry?'

'Oh just—I thought perhaps you wouldn't want to bother. Busy and all that.'

He was making an awkward laughing noise.

'Silly of me,' he said.

Indeed it was. Something evidently was up. And now he suddenly said:

'Eve's here.' The tone of his voice was too inconsequent. He forced himself to brighten up as he showed me in.

'An individual with one thirst!' he managed.

Eve rose to shake hands while he poured me a drink. I had expected an effusion of apology, some sort of brisk jollity to offset the nuisance of it all. But Eve seemed genuinely disturbed. As she shook hands, she blushed. She said quietly, quickly:

'I don't know what to say about all this.'

She looked over at Harry's back, and then fluttered

a quick glance at me—almost an appeal. One would have thought something quite different was at stake. It was uneasily out of keeping, and I began heartily:

'The best thing to say is nothing at all. Couldn't be helped . . . could it? Do let's forget it and talk of brighter things. . . .'

But what brighter things? I racked my mind. They were both looking at me, Harry humbly quizzing his brow and extending but holding back my drink not to interrupt what hopefully I was to say. Eve too stood waiting. I racked my mind. And then lamely blurted:

'You're not at the Club tonight?'

'Club?'

'That place you took me to—The Seventy or whatever it was.'

'Oh, we don't always go.'

We were sitting down. Eve propped herself on the edge of a pale settee as though it might poison her: Harry had gone over to the electric fire, switched a bar off, and now was over there again kicking it on. He said: 'No, that's Eve's sink of iniquity.'

Another desperate pause.

Harry made a laughing face.

This was getting us nowhere.

'And Audrey!' I brightly said. 'With her raving bloodlust?'

Harry cleared his throat, I saw him shoot out first one leg and then the other to pull up the creases of his trousers: then he leaned forward and tapped with his hands an empty pipe. His jaw lowered casually to say:

'Audrey? Mm. You know, Audrey's keeper's been very kind—she's driving Eve down tomorrow.'

He paused. Then: 'They're going early.'

67

Suddenly I saw that Harry was lying.

He sat making a fortress of himself, he had taken a long breath to do this and he was doing it very badly. It was shocking.

I glanced across at Eve. She was staring at him, she had forgotten me and her face hung blank with a sort of pain. She made a little movement of restraint with her hand.

'We don't think Eve's Aunt's in a very bad way,' he went on. 'Nothing serious, but . . .'

'Oh Harry! No!'

Her voice was low. But it cut in so suddenly Harry stopped. She began to speak quickly: 'No, Harry, I can't let you say that. You can't do it, darling—no!' She turned to me: 'I must get this straight. Martie isn't driving me down. My Aunt isn't ill. I had to have an excuse . . .'

Harry began: 'Now Eve, I'll handle this. . . .'

I muttered about it not mattering to explain, it was her affair. But she went on:

'Somebody rang up an hour ago. About a party. Harry talked to them. Somehow Martie got mentioned. It turns out she's away, so she couldn't have driven me down, so . . . it's so silly of me . . . I was just explaining to Harry when you came . . .'

She was plainly very upset.

'Cheer up,' I said, 'I'm sure you've got a good reason for it all. There's no need to explain.'

Harry muttered: 'None at all . . . that's right. . . .'

But Eve shook her head impatiently:

'No, you're both in this, there's no point in telling Harry and then Harry having to explain. I won't have that.'

We tried to object again—but now she was up and walking about the room as she talked. Pathetically it looked as if she were really trying to find a way out of the room—but she came up against a wall, a closed door, a window at every turn.

'I should have told you both long before. All this pretence of shopping . . .'

She stubbed out her cigarette decisively.

'I haven't got a passport,' she said. 'There!'

And now she looked from one of us to the other straight in the eye—it seemed almost triumphantly.

Triumph, or defiance, upon a puzzling minor matter. It was ridiculous, she sat there looking absurdly tragic —her pale eyes wide with appeal, her hands gripped tensely on the settee, her whole figure again too young for her dress, again something of the schoolgirl caught out. I began, despite myself, to feel angry, bored.

Harry frowned, and shook his head. He tried to smile: 'But why on earth didn't you tell us before? Did you forget?'

'Forget? How could I?'

'But darling—there's still time to get one. What's the—'

'You don't understand—'

'I don't see what on earth all the palaver's about.'

'I'm not *allowed* to have a passport. The police have confiscated it.'

'The police?'

'Yes. The *police*.'

Harry's face fell open, shocked: for a second only he looked frightened. Then he was full of concern for Eve, he was leaning forward and stuttering for an explanation.

69

If anything, I was pleased at this turn. The little lady had something behind her after all. A moment before she had looked absurd—and that is never pleasant: now what she had to say might solve much of the previous disquiet I had felt about her. And there was that curious tautness that charges the air when someone confesses to you a lie—a feeling almost that you yourself are really guilty.

'I wanted to tell you before but I didn't dare,' Eve said. She frowned and looked guiltily at Harry. 'Oh, I knew you'd understand—but I didn't want to have to make you. I suppose I just didn't want to tell.'

'Well'—she took a breath, sighed it, as if it was an old story that hardly merited the telling: 'It was at a time I was modelling furs for—oh who was it? Solly Green? I forget—anyway I wasn't earning much and I had horrid digs. I used to be miserable in the evenings and so I often went with another girl to a club she knew, just to sit somewhere really. Anyway it was there I met those people. I hadn't the faintest clue who they were. They seemed quite nice boys— and they were well off, perhaps I should have seen they were too well off for the time they had on their hands. Still, they were foreigners, a girl could have taken them for importers-and-exporters. Boys I say— they were men really. Thirty-ish.'

It would take too long, it would be too confusing to write down exactly how Eve told us that story. Had it weighed with her less she might have given us the point first. But she was intent on telling all—she described in detail many meetings and appearances and hours and streets and conversations that hopelessly retarded her point. But Harry was her real audience. And through all the fog of her detail he nodded and hummed, and his eyes opened and he frowned and he sometimes set his jaw with displeasure. He was consistently startled. All she said brought new pictures to his mind, pictures of her past, astounding hours that he would like to have possessed and had never even known of.

Eve had met two men in a club. They had taken her and her friend to Paris for the weekend. They were pleasant young men, they seemed simply to have been out for a good time of what Eve called 'the right' and not 'the wrong' kind. They also had a little business in Paris. On the return journey, coming off the boat at Dover, the young men had told the two girls to go on —they themselves had to stay back for a piece of missing luggage. So Eve and her girl friend had passed through the customs alone, and they had all met again in the train afterwards. It had been a lovely weekend: and it was repeated three or four times. Four times to be precise, and on the last occasion not only Eve's suitcase but her coat was searched and in one of the large outside pockets several little packets were found. She had never seen them before.

The customs office had opened one of them and had looked instantly serious. So—she didn't know where they had come from? It was her coat, wasn't it? If she didn't know, who then did? Then by a good stroke of fortune she caught sight of one of her gentlemen peering in at the other end of the customs shed. She pointed and said: 'I must ask my friend.' The customs officer had looked round just in time to catch the face retreating, he had sung out with authoritative joy: 'Who, *him*?'—and then they had all spent a long time speaking to senior officers in little wooden rooms.

Harry could no longer restrain himself. He was very frightened for her. Horror of the worst made his mouth curl like a bad taste.

'For God's sake, Eve—what was it?'

I too had a distasteful vision—the little white powders, the addict's seedy room, the ordinary faces with tragically dull eyes.

But Eve said:

'Lenses.'

I felt depressed. Drugs might have been distasteful, but they were an exciting idea: watches might even have enlivened the moment, there is something jolly about watches—men with dozens of wrist-watches up each arm or bangling beneath the wool-pipe of each thin leg like a dancer's jewelry. But lenses! Commercial lenses, lenses with a sawdust smack of the wholesale—with a value apparent only on the pavements of the lens market.

And those crossings, that Paris, those clubs! Visions of a callow Eve, pretty and young and wide-eyed, accepting the shabby graces of flash Channel-crossers. Their smooth-checked clothes, uniform of national indignity. The vista of the huddled third-class deck— nuns, scouts, schoolboys, and the mother with a daughter at Vincennes. But Eve and her boys in the first-class bar—where the monde clutching their cartons of cigarettes gulped down strong beer and cognac against the speed of the ship's engines. Eve's boys drinking only cordials—a crooked abstinence to keep the mind keen, abstinence of the knacker's tea-bar. And then the train, grinding slow through Amiens, to be met at the rickety Nord by a low little grey Peugeot.

'There we were—searched!' Eve was saying. 'And you should have seen what they found—packets all over us. I don't know whether Betty had more than me or me more than Betty.'

I looked at Harry, but there was no laughter. I sneered the smile off my lips, and thought about for something to say. Eve was going on:

'All in our bags too, wrapped in our clothes, little tissue paper packages . . .'

And I said unthinking: 'But how did they get the stuff into your packing? You had your own bags?'

'Our packing?'

Eve looked mildly surprised, as though a servant unsummoned had entered the room.

My tongue nearly came off. I looked quickly at Harry—and then wished I had not. He had realized. I hoped he was too troubled to notice. But of course he did. He would probably remember every detail of Eve's confused story long after she had forgotten.

'Oh, one or other of those fellows must have visited our bags during the crossing. On the boat while we crossed.'

'On the boat? Crooks? Out in the open?' Harry said. He said it bitterly, bitterly but hopefully.

Eve looked away from Harry and straight at me. Her voice was cool with scorn:

'I know what you're thinking,' she said.

Turning to Harry again, disdaining me utterly, without a pause she went on to describe what the excise officers had done. Thus in a second I was censured. And Harry and she were welded together, president censors. I felt hurt—and thankful.

'The upshot of it,' said Eve, 'was a court case and

those two were deported. But Betty and I had our passports taken away.'

She added thoughtfully: 'And that's why I haven't got a passport.'

Harry was plainly relieved. He went over to her and took her by the shoulders: 'You poor old thing,' he said. He was talking to a child more than a woman.

Eve hung her head, then looked up at him trustfully. He said: 'Well, it's not so bad, is it? How long ago, by the way?'

'Oh, I don't know. Years.'

Then as though it had become a guessing game and he had the answer: 'Two years?'

'And you haven't applied since?'

She shook her head.

Harry laughed, he gave her a little pat on the shoulder: 'In which case the doyens of law and order may be constrained to render.'

That was a shock. Both to Eve and to me—but in different ways.

Eve started—it was plain this had never occurred to her. But curiously, as though she had failed at the guessing game she only said: 'It may have been only one year.' She seemed neither eager to be forgiven nor anxious for the law to be 'constrained to render.'

To me, that phrase of Harry's brought the Camberley I knew best back to the room. For the last half hour he had not been there. There had been a man new to me, a frightened man, a man making a big fuss over a small matter. I was glad at the return of my facetious Harry. I was glad the anguish of domestic discussion was past.

In how many rooms do we sit, friends of the family, listening to problems that have no conflict, whose only need is to be *talked over*—as though in fact they had only to endure a process of cooking. There is nothing that cannot be solved by perhaps a single telephone call the next morning. But this tasty confection must be braised by the tongue: it must be basted, it must be turned right over. And in any case the result is served cold next day.

Yet one sits on and listens, a well-known old waiter, with neither an interest in the dish nor the authority to interpose a finger. Evenings as the friend of the family!

VI

THE blue Mediterranean sky blazed down, it was like a great domed lazuli compress stifling the breath of life. No wind. No wave. The sea glittered flat blue, the blue compress clung hot all around, blue sky and blue sea. It was a week later; and I was bored, bored, bored.

Bored with sitting about the bays round Cassis, bored with dragging my lonely old bones from place to place in the sun.

I had left London on the arranged day, and left Eve and Harry behind. Eve had continued to be evasive on the matter of a passport, Harry had not been able to get her to the authorities. She seemed frightened: she had hedged. I wondered why—but I decided to forget them. And not fancying the anticlimax of a journey abandoned, I had come down south by easy stages. Now I was looking for somewhere to settle down for the Spring to work.

But that is not easy, alone. The old trouble recurs. Should one settle here—in this indolent little port, elegant and comfortable but perhaps a shade too quiet? Or—just round that cape making secrets of the calm blue water—is there another port a little better? What of the evenings? What about someone to talk to? What about adventure?

Sniffing round the quays, sipping up the cafés, indecision turns to panic and panic to exhaustion; exhaustion to boredom. On the face of it life looks fine. The sun is out, the sea is sparkling. Agaves sprout their demon blue, cactus abounds, there are palms and oleander. The food is good, if rough. The wine an acid pleasure. But is not . . . is not the sun too hot, or too still, or too something? Will it not beat on day after day changeless, cloudless, breathless? And was that such a fascinating conversation in the bar last night, with that fisherman barman . . . was it not simply about prices, costs of living? And now those interesting newcomers there, rakish and smart out of their car and in their linen clothes, chattering down their cool drinks, buying papers and whiling the morning—they look interesting, the girls nubile and the men nonentitous . . . nice to meet? Well—why not go over? Shy? Nonsense. What's there to lose? Then in a little while perhaps? Time enough? And what to do with this Time? Sit with eyes fixedly averted? Reading so hard you see no words? Thrumming in the head? Squinting away up the street, away from them, pretending to see a friend? . . . Feeling, in fact, that they already suspect your interest and because of this—which you want—making sure they see you don't want to have anything whatsoever to do with them.

All such old ills plagued me during those sunlit days. To be alone is to be suspected of wishing not to be alone: a suspected intruder: sponger: bore. Meanwhile the sun shone relentlessly, the beauties sparkled, the saucers on the café tables rose, the pink-washed streets were too many times traversed, too many papers were read. And all around beauties of the sea and flower and plastered wall overwhelmed with their perfection—crying, 'Unused, unused! We cry to be used!'

Looking up into the hot blue, shading my eyes

77

against the slow-sweating glitter, I began to dream of mists and rain. I smelled fog. I remembered a February morning in England when I sat warm in sudden spring sunshine, while the lawn in front was whitely encrusted with frost; the earth hard, a keen fresh smell of frost in sap-warming sunlight. Finally I could stand it no longer. I remembered Roddy Meredith. And without wiring, for I had no idea of his hotel, took the train to Marseilles: Arles.

It was not difficult to find him. He was sitting out on the Lices. At tables nearby, Arlesian aficionados talked with their toreros. One bullfighter, a slender thin young man, sat still beardless but with all the holy, square-shouldered pride of Spain. It was Spanish there; but without the black and brown of Spain, with the blue and rose of France imposed.

'Hello, Roddy!'

He jerked his head up and very nearly expressed surprise: 'Morning,' he said. 'Coffee?'

We sat and talked lazily, the blue sky flooded above in new sympathy. I liked Roddy, despite his many artificialities. They scarcely needed to be taken as seriously as they often are. He had charm, a desire to please, and he listened well. He liked to laugh, and took no pattern of life too seriously. He was the very opposite of what the cinema presents as the desirable male—that fine morose superman who makes a virtue of surliness, who snaps and growls his longfaced way into the hearts of our millions. The desire to please is too often taken for servility. A hair'sbreadth manœuvre, too easily it can simply grin and simper and nod. To fulfil its function it must be rationed; and this Mr. Meredith easily and with reticent charm managed.

He could, if and only when necessary, fight and growl. But he never made a virtue of it.

So he was pleasant company for a day or two. We saw not too much of each other, and more than too little. We strolled in the warm evenings down the moist garden of the Alyscamps, where stone and vegetable best mix, stone of coffins and a green avenue of great and holy quiet. We watched a mithraic frolic with lyre-horned Camargue bulls in the great moonlit arena; we tasted the dove-grey benison of Trophime's pale roof. I stayed in a hotel where all night a dozen thumbsize beetles pushed balls of picnic-paper about the floor. Roddy avoided Van Gogh. I refused to sit on the planeflecked Boulevard des Lices, ruined by the great traffic that all day thundered past. We did many things—and one day we took a bus into the 'mysterious' Camargue to pass the day at Les Saintes Maries de la Mer.

It is this that I am really getting to. For there Roddy by chance told me something most curious about Eve. I have digressed enough—it is unnecessary to this story to describe my own troubles on the coast or our good time at Arles: except in some measure to indicate both the passage of time and the fact that Eve was forgotten. There was no reason why she should not be. She was simply a girl, charming enough, who had acted in an illogical manner—and that is not extraordinary. A girl who happened by chance to be engaged to an old friend in whom I no longer had much interest. So time must drift, time must harden, time must sigh its true length on a stage draped with people doing next to nothing.

But lying on the pebbled beach at Stes. Maries I found myself idly returning again to thoughts of Eve—

and murmured to Roddy, to the choppy little sea, what a perplexing girl she seemed to be. And suddenly I was remembering his raised eyebrows, his expression of mischief when he had seen me with her so long ago at that plastery little club. I turned on my elbow and asked the piece of face beneath his tilted hat what he had meant by it.

His hat tilted sideways as he turned a little to look at me. He looked sly. 'You wonder what I meant?' he asked, pretending not to believe me.

'Mm.'

'And you wonder, I suppose, why she's not down here with you?'

'With Harry.'

'Who's Harry?'

'The man she's engaged to. You met him that night. Tallish, moustache, sort of business man—' I found it difficult to describe him. I could only think of those advertisements for overcoats. I found myself murmuring the word 'clipped' and stopped.

But he remembered. And his lips lost interest. 'Oh, him. Vaguely.'

'He's an old friend of mine.'

'Really now?'

He seemed to be falling asleep again. The sea drove in with little waves on to the concrete, a concrete telegraph pole scudded above against a lonelier, paler blue sky—for it was not tropical on that flat delta, it was more like the south coast of England, concrete and windy and snapshot blue. There was a bungalow desolation about, it was no place to sleep and I wanted to talk. I passed over Harry and prodded about with a piece of bleached driftwood.

'Come, come. She's not the only one. Hundreds of people who've never had anything in their lives . . .'

'But she has had! Plenty. In a different way, perhaps. She threw up an ample, pleasant life in the country—which she herself looks back on with a certain longing, she told me herself . . .'

'She threw up a basement in Burnt Oak. And not so long ago, either . . .'

'Burnt Oak?'

'She was brought up there by an aunt.'

'But why—*why* does she say all this? She's a good-looking girl, in herself she's got a lot—'

'You know as well as I do that *that* makes no difference. I tell you, she's never had anything. But she's lived on the fringe of people who have. For instance . . .' —he seemed to ponder—'has she ever said: "I've always had money. Not a lot, you know. But I've always had *some*. It's nice to have always been able to get some money, isn't it?" Now has she ever told you that one?'

As he said that, I heard the exact words as they had come from Eve's mouth. I remembered the odd light satisfaction with which she had said it.

'Well,' said Roddy, 'if you ever hear that one— beware! Or shed a tear. It only means the opposite. It's the dream condition of a breaker-opener-of-gasmeters, a five-bob-from-mother's-bag girl. Just to *have money* is nearer her knuckle than all the other dreams of yachts and princes. Of course you'll get the yachts and princes too. But that one means the most.'

Just then a dog did come racing up, wet and ratlike. It stood shaking itself, legs wide and firm as tent-ropes, too near us. But Roddy was too engrossed, he went on:

'Have you ever gone into a tea-shop and ordered something for eightpence with your belly hanging out for a one-and-sixpenny rissole? And done this dressed up to the nine, dressed up to kill the fringe you live on—your hosts who are chumping up chickens at the dinner *after* which you are invited?'

We went quiet for a moment. Then I said: 'But hell, she's all right now. Why go on with it?'

Roddy threw a straggle of wood scimitaring down the beach. The dog looked crazily grateful, went bounding after it, barked sideways, lost its direction and went sniffing and wagging in the wrong place. The little white waves growled in at it, ceaseless white terriers. Roddy said at length: 'Oh, I suppose she's a bit of a snob too.'

But emphatically Eve was not a snob. It took the spoken word to remind me how badly this matched her. 'There's something more than that . . .' I began.

'She likes to play at kings and queens.'

But this was Roddy's own failing. He had a profound, and pathetically distant, adoration of the aristocratic. Or failing that, of the very rich. Now I knew he might be wrong. His intuition might tell him more about a woman than mine could—but finally he got it twisted up with his narcissist self. But I said to him:

'Well—it's incredible. And she's certainly covered up her tracks very well with friend Harry.'

'They do.'

The dog came back with the wrong piece of wood, which Roddy refused.

'Harry wouldn't give a damn,' I said, 'where she

came from. But it'll be a difficult moment when he does find out—I mean, he'll be hurt by the deception and so on . . .'

'Before he does, there'll come a fine day when she'll confess. It'll be dramatic, they'll both be moved. It depends entirely on her whether that happens just before or some time after she hooks him.'

I congratulated him on knowing so much. And now please would he tell me what the devil had made her slink out of a perfectly good holiday in the sun? That didn't fit in anywhere. I mentioned the passport. He laughed and shook his head.

'I should say . . . she's not quite sure that she's hooked him. Or that she's not sure that she finally wants to hook him. Anything, her instinct says, might happen before hooking time. And to go away is somehow a drastic measure, to bed or not to bed.'

'You don't like her very much, do you?' I grumbled.

'I do, I do,' he said, throwing that dog another stick. 'But facts must be faced. She can't let her hair down with me and pull it over my eyes at the same time. She's a nice girl. But ordinary.'

I thought again of that time in the park—that time when the cavalry had glittered past—when he had been so astonished that I did not leap to help my friends. And murmured, more to myself than to him:

'What, I wonder, should we do. . . .'

Roddy shook his head at the dog and sank his head back on the beach. 'Nothing. Let it ride, let it ride.'

Eve and Harry were, of course, not his friends.

'Well, I don't think in the first place you're right about her,' I said. 'I think there's much more to it. I don't know whether I should let it go at that. . . .'

'Let it ride, let it ride. . . .'

He was falling asleep.

I too. Despite the Channel wind, I felt the sun's heat taking me. I closed my eyes and murmured to myself: 'It's too complicated. I'm here and they're there. It's too much to ask. I'll—let—it—ride.'

VII

IT rode.

Sometime in June, when I found the right hotel and was working in earnest, I got an invitation to the wedding. And when I returned to London in September they were settled in their new house in Surrey.

I went down for a day in the guise of a tardy wedding guest—and about three weeks later Harry rang me up again. We chatted into the vulcanite, paused, began again, and I kept wondering what next to say—for he had produced no purpose for his call. Then it came. He stammered a little, then it flooded out quick:

'Look, old man—I'm going to ask you a favour. It may sound silly, you may not like it, but you're the only one somehow I can really ask and I do want your help in this. Badly, old man.'

I told him to go on, he seemed to take a breath more than pause:

'It's about Eve. She's visiting someone—this afternoon, late. A friend of hers. To put it short—I want you to go too.'

'Me? But do I know this friend? . . . What can I do?'

'Look, old man, if you've got anything on, I'm going to ask you to put it off. I'm in dead earnest. Whatever it is. Will you . . .?'

'I suppose . . . yes. But do explain—where do I meet her? What for?'

'You don't meet her, that's it. I want you to watch where she goes and, well—what she does.'

It was difficult to believe. His voice was pathetic, I knew he was badly worried. But what a proposition! I could not help myself:

'I thought there were agencies for that sort of thing?'

'Don't misunderstand, old man.'

'What have I misunderstood?'

'I couldn't do that to her. That's why I'm asking you. . . .'

'But you could do it to me?'

'Yes.'

That was all he said.

'You mean seriously you want me to follow her and spy for you?'

'Yes.'

'But . . . but—Harry, what's it all about?'

'I can't tell you. Not now. Even if I did it wouldn't help—yet. Look—she's going to visit a house, I'll tell you where, on the embankment, Chelsea. At five-thirty. You'll see me drive her there. Drop her. And I'll be back to pick her up.'

'But I don't see . . .'

'I want you to watch what she does. Christ, this sounds awful.'

'And you . . .?'

'I can't do it myself.'

'It seems very much in the family to me.'

'I can't wait about there, if she thought I was spying about, if she saw from the window—it'd break too much up. . . .'

'And me?'

'There's no reason why you shouldn't be there. Chance. Looking at the river. I don't know. Anyway, don't show yourself, that's only in case she happened to see . . .'

'Steady. I haven't agreed to this.'

'Please—you don't know how important—'

'I don't.'

'I've *got* to know what she does.'

'How would I tell, looking at a blank house? It *is* a house?'

'If you like, if it would help your feelings, I know this is awful for you—if you like you needn't tell me what happens. It can be up to your discretion.'

'So now you don't want to know?'

'I can't explain. But I do mean that—it can be your discretion.'

That word 'discretion' was ominous, it sounded heavily responsible—like 'honour'. But I saw that at the same time it gave me some sort of an exit. And—it must be admitted—I was curious. And I think it was that curiosity—the cold, perhaps contemptible curiosity of the observer detached from life—that finally made me agree. By profession, and thus by nature, I had to observe more or less unseen. And here it was, offered on a plate. I agreed.

'And when,' I said drily, 'shall I use my discretion on you?'

'*Please* don't say it like that.'

I heard again the anxiety in his voice and was sorry.

'Well, Harry—when?'

'It can't be till tomorrow.'

'Shall I phone?'

'Could you come down? For the day? The night?'

I said the day. Now, with his request granted, he

began to apologize for it. His relief was so great he nearly forgot to give me the address before we rang off.

When three weeks before I had gone down to their new house, I was impressed by a mature atmosphere of married content. I had gone down fearfully—as I said, in duty as a belated wedding guest—with Roddy Meredith's words ringing in my ears. I expected trouble. I found peace.

They had the ample size of house in which people of Harry's income still manage to live well despite their complaints of high taxation and restricted business. "Uplands", if it was not built on rock, was built on expenses. It was a six-bedroom affair built in the twenties, retired enough in its three acres of rhododendron, birch and fir. But retired only in that it was hidden among trees—in itself it was a formidable amalgam of many telling styles: one felt that the railways had managed a direct line falsewards into the Wars of the Roses.

In this house Eve had plainly settled down to work in earnest. When I found them—it was a Sunday morning—Harry was in his shirtsleeves tidying the garden and Eve in trousers was measuring space for carpeting in one of the rooms. There was no attempt to dress up and receive me. They were still intent on receiving the house. Eve cooked lunch—for no amount of expenses could solve the servant problem—and generally she hustled about, houseproud and happy, the whole day. It seemed to be no energy of nervousness. She was engrossed. I remember walking out onto the lawn for a moment—it had just showered, and the dried-out air of September was freshened again, rain-drops flashed gold on a few scattered leaves and on the long-stalked autumn flowers—I remember thinking what a comfort it was that she had settled in so well. After all she was capable, and she was loving it. It put the lie to all Roddy had said, and I wondered whether, if his tale of a near-pathological condition had ever been true, whether such people were able in fact to take a deep breath and thus revive. I looked back and through the dusk of the french windows and saw the two of them sprawling at last in chairs and laughing at Harry's attempt to open, sitting, a bottle. Plainly, Eve had revived.

How should one describe their placid energy, their energetic peace? Perhaps by the absolute incuriosity with which I was asked how it had been down in France? Content with a general answer, they were already absorbed in some plan for a gardener. Or by a kind of pride in Eve's movement when she went to get me a new towel? A movement almost nonchalant, that said: 'We have clean towels, many, for this is a household.' Or by Harry's contented talk of a golf-course nearby, of the fast train service to London, and of the proximity of the terminus to his office? Or by Eve's tired, pleased stretch when she grumbled: 'Well —I suppose I must go and feed the chickens'?

Later on that day the woman Martie—who lived nearby and who in fact had first suggested to them the house—drove up in a small black saloon. She hallo-ed at us from the drive: and then, on seeing me, brightly said: 'And what do you think of my babies?' I looked vainly into her car. But she meant Eve and Harry, of course. It confirmed everything.

And now this unpalatable telephoning of Harry's.

At some minutes before half-past five I was leaning
over the river wall, a thick plane-tree between me and
the balconied old Chelsea house I was employed to
watch. Low tide, the river muddy and slow—my
spirits the same. Unusually, I was wearing a hat: and
this ridiculous precaution, though it might have de-
ceived a friend, pressed selfconsciously onto my fore
head. All eyes I felt were on me.

The evening traffic sped along behind, a stream of
a thousand cars each with a person fanning out of this
London to some home far beyond. One glimpsed a
sight of a face, and saw a household inside each car. I
saw many—I had to keep turning to peer round my
tree in case this or that car lowering its speed might be
Harry's. But I was early, or they were late—and time
and again I turned back to the forlorn river, to the
scrappy breeze that rippled an evening cold across it,
to the barges and the tugs that no longer looked busy
and plucky but now soot-poor and tired. I had plenty
of time to reflect not only on my own position there—
but also on what it must have cost a man of Harry's
simple integrity to ask me to come.

But at length—with none of the dramatic surge of
arrival I had expected—his car dribbled away from
the others and stopped quietly by that house. Eve came
crouching out, stood for a moment talking to him—
and then turned to the portico. For some moments she
stood on the steps—it looked sadly—and watched him
away: then turned not up the steps but down again
to the pavement. She walked quickly off to the left.

I stood for a moment startled, for I had taken up my position firmly—then realized I had to leave it and follow. And Eve walked very fast. She walked fast round the corner, jigging high on her heels. But round the corner I nearly bumped into her, she had slowed to a stroll, her head down and considering something. I had to stop, to lengthen the distance between us. It was a street of grimed plaster houses with dirty bright-painted doors. I stopped and peered intensely at a window-box derelict of flowers. It was some time before I saw a woman's face, old and outraged, staring at me from the darkness of the room beyond. I began walking again. Words formed in case Eve turned: 'Why, hello stranger!' and 'Fancy meeting you!' I could think of nothing better. Once I thought suddenly that I myself might call out, I could take the initiative and deflect whatever she was going to do! But of course that could only postpone to another day what was going to happen—and like a muffled dog I plodded on.

She was in no hurry. She paused at a shop selling antiques, I had to stop too and gaze into a white inferno of electric irons and radio sets. She lingered over a bookshop, I was given a laundry window with nothing but myself mirrored in the glassy green paint. And this went on up one street and down another. Corners were the worst. Would she disappear? Would I get round too soon? . . . Then suddenly she looked at her wrist-watch and began to hurry. She looked up at the name of the street, crossed it, and went into a tea-shop.

I hung about a few minutes in case she had gone in there just to buy something. Or to find someone. But soon it seemed otherwise. And soon I took courage and walked quickly past. Twice then luck favoured me. My eyes just topped the ring and crinkles of the top of a halfway net curtain: and her back was turned. She was sitting at a table alone.

I walked on wondering now what was to happen, and decided all I could do was to watch the door and see who went in. Once or twice, as the minutes passed, people clanged open the handle of that glass door. A worn, erect old man, dragging his feet; a pretty girl unsexed in a strange green uniform; a young man with a dark skin and dark hair in a dark brown suit. Each time I walked past, I looked in. None of them sat with Eve. Each time I stopped and pretended to study the menu stuck behind the window. In pale blue ink it offered plaice or croquettes, charlotte pudding and coffee extra. In one corner there was a coloured drawing of a turkey gobbling among a peal of churchbells and a piece of heather. Standing out there in the cold, collar up, I could only think: 'Gobble! Gobble! Gobble!' I looked up and saw that the place was called 'Turkee's Delite'. Who in the hell was Turkee? The nickname of some cheery old Chelsea-ite, greying and game, mummy-joy of bed-sitting-room parties, all buns and bum and big blue slacks? And what did that waitress think of my sour street-face pressing in at the menu? Pity for one who could not afford it? But contempt pulled down her beautiful lips. Once suddenly she started forward at me, and I slunk back into the dusk.

Eve had been sitting there for a full twenty minutes. A policeman walked past, turned a while later and walked back. He looked at me. I pretended to look at a watch I had not got, and looked up and down the street for the person for whom I was so hopelessly waiting. It is difficult to look at a policeman at any time, but then it was worse. I tried to decide that he pitied me for the girl who had not come.

Up above, the sky was darkening. A sad scrappy sky, with clouds not dark nor light, colourless, nor even quite colourless enough to define itself: it was nothing, dishwater between the lightless roofs of this straight long street through which buses sometimes dragged and a few people walked quickly. A sky and a street that made Londoners leave. Once a pale salmon streak shot in above from the setting sun, made a sudden furnace of a red chimney, and flickered out. That was all. No dogs, no cats: those infrequent buses, all with the same number, rumbled past a request stop without hesitation.

In that tea-shop there was a clock. And now and again when I looked in, the hands had surprisingly changed their position. I will not say time went slowly: I was too perplexed for time to drag. It was just sad. Sad and long and empty. For nothing happened, nothing. Whoever she expected simply did not turn up. She simply sat on there alone for—a full two hours. Sat among the sad conclave of men at their lonely suppers—for most were men, office-drained, alone with books or newspapers, fearful and cheerful with the waitress who despised them, eating their suppers slowly for fear of returning to their beds too early.

But it was plain Eve expected no-one. She took no interest in the time, she shot out no wrist-watch nor looked at the clock above her. Sitting erect at her chair, colourful and a little mysterious among these men, she ate whatever she had without taking any interest in the room. Once, with the startling ease of a soignée woman for an unmade bed, she picked up a used newspaper from the chair opposite. She ordered another cup of tea and read this from the front page through.

And I—but thirst, cold and tobacco mouth are dull things to talk about. And they do not come into the story. Suffice it to say that at twenty minutes to eight Eve rose, paid her bill and left. She walked straight back to that house on the embankment and stood in the porch—she might have been sheltering from the rain—for the last ten minutes before Harry arrived.

When the car at last drew up she came slowly down the steps, took a last and most longing look back at the house, gave her head the breath of a toss and entered the car. They drove off.

VIII

THOSE at Oxley who own cars use a large main line station that skirts what once was the nearby market town. This station, with its bridges and its red brick and its bright green paint, sees the morning assembly of men of business. For those, like myself, who do not own cars and who perhaps fear the station-yard battle for one of the few dowager taxis—for those a branch line runs to a little frilled hermitage of a station called Oxley Rise. To this on the next day I travelled.

It was a fine September morning. Coming out from under the fawn canopy of that little station, the sun shone on a chalk cutting still green with weeds. Birds that had not already moved south sang. There was a smell of coming ripeness in the air, but all was still green and white under the blue.

Away from the railway cutting the hills abruptly ceased. Only the Heath stretched ahead. Bracken and heather, across which the smooth-tarred motor-roads cut cleanly, and where little silver birches wisped like pen drawings against the distant dark of Surrey fir. I took a sandy track into the bracken—and there far off saw the figure of Harry. We waved to each other; then each of us strode forward, awkwardly scanning to left and right of us—submarine commanders periscoped in a sea of green heath. At another time I would have been glad he had short-circuited my arrival like this. But I was apprehensive—although my news was, on the face of it, good.

As soon as we had greeted each other he turned his eyes away, and said just: 'Well?'

I told him what had happened.

I expected him to show some sort of relief that nothing disastrous had happened: or that Eve's plan, whatever it was, had failed. I was most unprepared for the growling little sob he made. Then he kept muttering to himself: 'Oh God.'

We walked on. At last he spoke: 'It's just as I thought.' He turned to me, his face was strained and miserable: 'You didn't notice her looking for anyone? Even in that shop?'

'I can't say that I did. Really, no.'

'Oh . . . hell . . .!'

Then he started speaking quickly: 'You'd better know about this now. It's driving me mad. I don't know what to do.

'You see—a few weeks back, just after you were down I think, she came to me and told me about a man she'd known before we were married. Oh, a long story. Some middle-aged bastard who had befriended her when she was broke at some time or other. She had been wandering alone on the embankment, he had been standing there and somehow they got talking. She described him to me—tall, iron-grey hair, courteous —and how he had asked her whether she'd like a lift home and how she said in what and there was this huge grey car—Hispano-Suiza or something. Anyway, he began to look after her—in a fatherly way, she said. Always courteous. Gave her dinner once a week, gave her money too. Developed a great affection for him . . . sort of fitted in as a father. He lived in that house in Cheyne Walk.'

He paused. 'Well, she swore nothing had gone on between them—I didn't ask her, but she went out of her way to emphasize that. . . . But now it was different, she said. Even a relationship of that kind couldn't continue now, she'd written to him about our being married, that it must be finished. Only—she wanted to see him once more to say goodbye, to thank him for ever and so on. Of course, I told her to bring the chap down—though I wasn't really too keen to see him. But she insisted it must stop.'

We had passed off the heath into a small wood, pine-needles matted us with quiet, the light between the flickering pines became a game of red indians. Harry said, dry in that quiet:

'Well, you were present at that final meeting.'

'But no-one turned up. . . .'

'There was no-one in the first place. It was all a bloody pack of . . . it was all make-believe.'

Of course, then I remembered what Roddy had told me on that beach. Harry went on:

'It's mad—but it's true.' Then he turned and said in a puzzled way, as if he were feeling for the place of a pain: 'She makes up these things, you know.'

I pretended:

'That's not so bad then—what are you grumbling about? You're let off without this mysterious father-stranger.'

'No, no. It's not only that. You don't see. She does it all the time. I've been getting wise to it quite a while. But now—look, if you can believe me, listen to this . . . We were opening one of her trunks that came down. We were there together. By chance a diary fell out of it. I happened to pick it up—it was unused. I remember thinking it'd come in useful, and then I saw it was dated six or seven years ago. I just left it there and thought no more.

'A week later I found it again, laid out where I should see it, and I picked it up again, I thought idly perhaps the days fitted in with the same dates this year. I opened it—and realized it was a different diary altogether. It was filled in. But then I saw the same smear of old red ink over the date-page—it seemed the same diary after all.

'It's hard to believe but—she'd filled in every page! She'd invented a whole year of her life. The whole thing—lunches at the Ritz, the Berkeley: men's names, Alec for three weeks, dinner with Michael, Paris with John and John's aunt: a month in the Pyrenees: scratchings out, additions, everything—even appointments for work, even that!'

I could hardly help smiling. It seemed an innocent enough game to play with oneself, and I told him so.

'I thought so too. I even thought how damned cleverly she'd done it. But I said nothing . . . and sure enough that evening she pretended to find it herself, chuckled over it, in the end tossed it over to me "to read all about her wicked past." I didn't know what to do, old man.'

His voice faltered. He seemed ashamed: 'So I had to play too. The two of us sitting there! That's a fine sane picture of married life, isn't it?'

We were out of that pine-wood, and the first houses were starting. Each stood back from the road, its family of windows guarded by well-kempt trees, glimpses only of each pantiled or mansarded or beamed façade and each air of private history.

'It's got so bad I can't believe a word she says,' Harry went on. 'That's the dreadful thing. Do you see what I mean? Whenever she opens her mouth and tells me what she's done or going to do, I—I have to turn my eyes away. It's dreadful to love some one so much and have to do that.'

I must have murmured something about exaggerating matters—but I was beginning to feel what he must be going through.

'They talk about living in a bad dream—and it's exactly that. Dreamlike. And bad. Yet . . . I know she's not bad. It's in a way the opposite. The whole thing's childlike, it's innocent. Apart from everything else—I'm put in the position of complaining of innocence.'

'Perhaps she'll get over it in time. . . .'

'No, old man. It's getting worse.'

We walked on past those houses brooding their peace.

'If she'd done these things she wouldn't hint at them. It's because she'd done nothing she has to make it up . . . it's pathetic—'

He turned angrily:

'As if she wasn't good enough for a—a bloody prince without all that. And she thinks she has to convince *me*. . . .'

It was difficult to say anything. I felt he had just better talk away. Besides, Eve was not all that much exceptional. Many women—and men too—make up stories to enhance their life. Perhaps not so many take matters as far as Eve had—yet the same impulse rules. But I must have mumbled something about not taking it so hard. One of those well-meant, impossible phrases. He turned at me:

'Hard?' he said. 'Hard? You seem to think it's some ordinary little row. I tell you it's different—this is our whole life. Realize that. Realize that we can't sit together and talk about the past or the present—or even the future. If she says she's going out to—even to drive over to Martie's damn kennels—I have to think twice before believing her. If we talk of going for a weekend away somewhere, I have to allow for some drama that'll prevent it. If we want to chat over what we've done in our lives—the way people do, the way people grow closer with that sort of way of finding out about each other—well then there I am facing her face, her clothes, the way she's sitting, all the things I love so much real in front of me and yet there it is, a dreadful sort of nothingness round her . . . does that convince you? Can't you see how ridiculous, no—how simply bloody tragic it is?'

His voice dropped, he paused and then muttered over again:

'I just don't know what I'm going to do.'

I said nothing, our shoes made a hard marching beat on the tarred road—alone, it felt like marching on to nowhere. He looked round to me—his eyes asking, a little humble smile on his lips. He said, he pleaded from that moustached, man's face:

'What *should* I do?'

'Do?'

'Should I have it out? Tell her I know?'

'Well . . .'

'We've never had a row.'

He went on:

'It's sure to hurt her. Remember when you were a kid—being found out? Hell, it punctures your pride, she'll feel . . . I don't want to humiliate her . . .'

'Someone's got to be hurt. Perhaps the sooner the less.'

'You see there's another thing—'

He frowned, and then I heard what always surprises so from a man like Harry: abstraction. Because a man seldom expressed himself, one thinks he never thinks. Then from out of a face it comes—one sees he certainly has been thinking. And one suspects, uncomfortably, that he has simply the good sense usually to keep abstraction in its place.

'There's another thing, I don't know whether in the end she's not right. I'm sure she half believes in all this herself. She lives in a world of what-do-you-call-it —make-believe—and I offer her what I believe is reality. But what is reality? How do I know—?'

Out of the corner of my eye I could see his homely, hairy tweed arm swinging: his hand gripped the handle of an unpolished stick: there were hairs on the hand, and his knuckles shone white through the rough sunburn. It looked real enough.

'How do I know,' he went on, 'that what I believe in, or do, is real? Hell, you see illusion all the time. You see an old sailor's eyes light up when he hears the pipe—and it's a damn silly sound—of a boatswain's whistle. You see a chap knocking on the door of his boss's office—frightened to death. You see an old girl in a new hat. All of them, they're believing in something quite unreal—but you can see by their faces they think it's real enough themselves. They're away in a dream of one sort or another. Ship, office door, they are all real in one sense: in the sense that you can touch them—though I've heard even that doubted. But what the people *think* is quite different. All of those three live in two ways, they can all go about doing things practically: yet still they'll be thinking in an unreal way. It's the same with Eve. She can do things. But she thinks up others. Only she doesn't need a hat or a navy to do it for her, she thinks them up herself. Why not?'

I said: 'But Harry there are degrees . . .'

'There are not. It's all the same. Put it another way. Suppose you see a young girl at her first dance, in her first dance frock and with the lights and the music making things romantic—would you give that girl a pair of magic middle-aged sensible spectacles to ruin her make-believe? No you wouldn't. Because you'd think: let her dream. Well damned if I can see any reason to disabuse Eve of her dream.'

'Apart from your own peace of mind, which . . .'

'Which might have to be my own affair.'

I thought that sounded too sacrificial.

'Heavens,' I said. 'It's only a matter of getting her to grow up. She's a woman now. It's just a kind of infantilism. Your analogy with a girl at her first dance is exact—'

'Get her to grow up? Fine . . . fine . . . speak to her as a sensible woman, eh . . .?' He just turned away and grunted: 'Call yourself an author!'

It would have been then, I feel, that I first began to realize—rather than to suspect and wish to avoid—the fact that he was not making a mountain from a molehill. It was serious. Yet on that bright morning, with the cosseting of the Surrey scene around us, with the assurance of tweed and the sound of our feet on the road—it was difficult to imagine that very much could be wrong with a world that so plainly intended to remain comfortably right. But it is exactly at times like this that one must remind oneself that the man in front is not the man you see: he is not the man with the tweeds and the grim stance and the clipped moustache: he does not see himself, he is inside himself, he is a pair of dark holes, the bone round his eyes, and the 'him' humming darkly down inside.

We passed a house of morning movement. From an upstairs window the sound of bathwater came gurgling clear across the gravel. Two figures in white flannels moved about a car glinting in the sun, they called up into the air: 'We're ready!' The bright rhythmic plap of a tennis ball came from somewhere behind trees. The house was a white and blue extravagance in Californian-Spanish style. Tudor beams were there to help. It did not look very real.

I began to say: 'Surely—illusion depends very much on degree? If you want any yardstick—as to what is bad or good—you can only relate it to other people. It's finally a social question. Same with all fantasy. If an illusion injures the society around it, then it must be righted. By righted I mean sorted towards whatever illusion the society itself indulges in.'

'And where does the injury begin and end?' Harry was asking—and then fortunately broke off, his hand was on his gate and he said quickly: 'Forget about it now. I'm sorry. We'll have to behave as if nothing's happened.'

So we entered the shallow drive of "Uplands", and there was Eve bent picking bits off flowers by the porch.

And the day passed enjoyably. Harry was determined to put a bright face on it, to keep that stiff upper lip. And perhaps Eve had satisfied herself for the time being—the resolute parting with her grey-haired protector had occurred only the day before. And the weather was fine.

It was a day in midweek. Between weekends—as it was between seasons. The garden seemed to be swept of summer by new air and light, new vistas appeared between the shrunk but unfallen leaves, the sun pretended to take on a more oblique, whiter slant. And to match this the midweek activities filled the air—there was a sweeping and a light business about the houses, a going and coming of tradesmen's vans, short escapades of little cars driven by single women, now the whine of an electric sweeper, now an opening of windows or a glimpse of laundry being carried upstairs. The pantiled liners were taking in provision for the weekend trip when father would take the bridge: among the rhodies a polishing and a stoking were abroad.

But in the afternoon, somewhere at four o'clock, silence dropped as forcefully as a siren. Tea-time. And there were indeed sirens—twice the high pipe of a whistling kettle whispered from the surrounding woods. And there among their trees and their different walls, unseen and hidden from each other, matronly muscles relaxed and virtuous minds sighed to smell the aroma, light as the shadow of a vase, of tea. And tea found us sitting in the drawing-room—the 'lounge', as Harry expressed it. Eve was settled with a wireless magazine and a bundle of socks beside her. The tea-trolley stood piled with the profound impedimenta of that so slender meal. The scene was calm.

And as we chatted quietly, the children's hour piped its little squeaks from a wireless whose homely yellow light glowed assurance. 'We hope to have the tee-vee soon,' Eve was saying, as she saw my eyes on the little light . . . but then there came a crunch of car-wheels on the drive outside. We all sat up stretching our necks like ventriloquist's dummies—to see through the window the top of a small saloon car.

'It's Martie!' cried Eve. She rose briskly, she took all those socks off her lap and rose at the same time, a graceful neat movement, as a woman rises with knees together.

Thus as six o'clock struck, Martie—Mrs. Milward-Jones—came laughing in with her sealyham Audrey and a tall spotted dog called Peter. 'They'll be all right, don't worry,' she breezed in her deep voice. 'Audrey's herself just now.' And so it seemed, for Peter paid no attention to her, he simply strolled over to the french windows and stood shivering his hindquarters at the garden; while Audrey flopped down panting on a rug in front of the cool autumn fireplace.

Martie was just telling us what she had been doing that day—she'd been over to the town and back, she'd got only three eggs from her seventeen hens, and she'd taken the 'other fellow' to the vet . . . when there came another grind of brakes on the gravel outside! It was something called the Roberts-is. And soon into that lounge there sauntered a tall, sad, elegant woman whose eyes turned downwards at the corners and whose mouth did the same, all on a sweet-tired note that stated: 'I was very beautiful once. I still am.' And her two sons—one a keen stern square young man in a blue flannel jacket and a green pork-pie hat, and the other small and crouched and sallow.

These people had been asked in for 'cocktails': and our peace was gone. Now there was general chatter: and, as happens, the subject remained near home. Names I did not know peopled like ominous wraiths the dusking room—the Fletchers, old man Doublejoy, and, with a reverent familiarity that suggested few really knew them, the Mordaunts of Hill Close. For lack of knowing them, one felt an unpardonable ignorance. The young man in blue flannels asked me if I was an 'Oxleyite': on my negative, he looked severely at his shoes. I was introduced to Mrs. Roberts as an author, and she was quick to ask me whether I did it on a typewriter or actually wrote it all out with a pen—before passing on to the dreadfulness of a row of workmen's cottages being built on the Heath. 'Oxley's not what it was,' they all agreed: just as people in remoter houses had agreed before the building of such as "Uplands". The name was seldom off their lips. 'You don't get that kind of thing in Oxley.' Or, with a knowing laugh: 'Trust Oxley for that.' Though none could have had any roots in the place, their election to live at Oxley had itself produced a fighting pride.

Suddenly Martie jumped up with alarm: 'Heavens! I forgot the pups! And he hasn't come yet!'

Something of an enigma. But it turned out that Martie had a couple of pups in a basket in the car, and that someone was calling that evening to see them. And no sooner had she strode out to the car and returned with a basket from which sniffed the stunned faces of two black and white puppies—than there

came a further ring at the bell, and I was being introduced to a portly red-faced man with black-rimmed
spectacles. Then Eve laughed: 'But of course—you
know each other!'

Together we touched hands and peered suspiciously,
neither sure, and mumbled our 'of courses'. Then it
turned out to be that Mr. Barnett whom I had met
the night that Audrey bit Roddy. He had come
down to buy a dog from Martie. It was a present,
he explained, to a young singer he had discovered.
'Something to keep her quiet,' he said, 'when she's
not singing.'

Harry, always on the move, brought us more of the
little cocktails. And the room rose to its chatter again.
Among those people Eve and Harry looked separate
and distinguished—perhaps simply by their normality,
their ordinary good looks. Distinguished from Mrs.
Roberts, leaning back in beautiful disfavour, drooping
her voice about, shedding a superior charm about . . .
what? Her husband a director of three tea companies?
Her house that was twice the size of others? Her
father, a General in Ceylon? . . . And distinguished
from the good doggy soul of Martie, booming goodwill from her spinster heart (Spinster? Many years ago
she had been married, but he had run away). Distinguished from those two young men, one keen and
fiercely paramount, the other charmless for life.
(Those two sat above the puppies. One puppy crouched
listless with bowed head, and the other tore bright-
eyed at the rug. Which were boys, which pups?) And
distinguished from old Barney, who in his prosperous
dark suit and his well-whiskied belly had travelled all
the way down that night to get a dog on the cheap.

And who was now prevailed upon to sit at the piano and sing his latest hit: *Sweet and Tender.*

'*Su-et and ten deer,*' Mr. Barnett sang wheezing his tenor through the sieve of sweetness. '*Su-et and ten deer,*' he sang, pudgy hands planting a tender minor seventh.

Harry winked at me. Barnett made every 's' a 'sh'. From some layer of snobbery, Harry did not much like him. He was only something from that club of Eve's. But I think Eve liked him, Eve had no snobbery in her: exactly as she had developed no set romantic tastes for herself, but welcomed most romance, so she had no tastes between people, but welcomed most of them—and now Harry whispered to me, his eyes amused:

'What do you think of that lot, eh?'

I remember laughing, though I rather liked this Barnett. He had a kind of dull brio. I said:

'It's wonderful how he believes in the stuff . . . look . . .'

'Believes in it? All that moon-June nonsense? Steady on, old man—he's only selling it.'

'I think he gets a real exaltation out of it, broadly as any poet on his plane gets out of writing—'

'Oh come, I don't know much about poetry and all that, not much good at it—but hell.'

'But you *are* "good at it"—in your way. Everybody's some kind of a poet. Look at Barney, look at his eyes, look at the tilted head—he's moved, he's exalted. Something's doing it to him. Only it's on a pretty simple plane—that's all.'

'It defeats *me*.'

'You listen to him talking about a "new number". He's doing more than sell it, he's believing and loving it.'

We were going on like that: and then Barnett came to an end. When he stopped there was a short silence, others had been talking but the sudden quiet of the piano stopping paused them. In this moment's uncertainty, Eve's voice came clear:

'Oh! I'd forgotten! I can't tomorrow—there's a—a funeral. . . .'

There was the usual muttering of sympathetic hush.

But Eve, unasked, went on: 'I feel I really must go . . . it's a—a very old friend. . . .'

Harry said in a dead direct voice: 'What funeral, Eve?'

She looked up at him sadly: 'I didn't want to bother you, darling. I feel I must go, it's over at Esher . . . a very, very old friend of the family. . . .'

I looked at Harry, his face grew unbearably dulled, his lips pressed in to contain himself. He looked tired, he said loudly in despair for the whole room to hear:

'Oh, *Eve* . . .'

Mrs. Roberts started up alarmed: 'I say my goodness gracious look at the *time*! I had no idea—we must *fly* . . . John! Roger! . . .'

Her two boys in their different ways rose. For a moment these three diverted what heavy thing had suddenly weighted the air, they made the room stand up, standing figures were everywhere shaking hands and waving and moving off. That tall spotted dog ran round and in and out like an eel wagging. Martie boomed: 'Down, Peter!' Harry saw them to the door.

Barnet sat down again and began strumming some other song. Martie had Peter by the collar, I handed my glass to Eve. When Harry came back he went straight to Eve, interrupted the pouring of my drink, said urgently: 'Eve, I've got something to say to you. Come out a moment.'

I tried to protest about my drink—anything to divert what had suddenly possessed him. But he was out of hand. He took her by the arm and led her out through the windows to the lawn. As Barnett sang, as Martie began to tell me about her puppies, I saw Eve and Harry out on the lawn—two figures in the evening glow gesticulating. I could hear no word of what they were saying. Isolated there in the dying day, they looked like figures in a silent film: for Harry was urgent, he was jerking as he spoke, and Eve made movements of a heroine dismayed. English, they gesticulated otherwise than with their hands; Harry kept moving the pose of his feet, his chin was now down on his chest, then abruptly up; Eve crossed her arms, uncrossed them and patted the back of her hair, then moved a hand to her neck—a gesticulation of poses. They were having a row. All the healing of the day was undone.

Then Barnett stopped playing and came over.

'Now let's 'ave a good look at these fellows,' he said, bending over at the puppies. The puppies, sleek and black and white, peered up with their small blind eyes. Their noses twitched upwards. Barnett wheezed down at them. 'First time old Barney's ever been sold a pup, eh?'

Martie laughed. 'Never been shold a pup,' Barnett repeated, crooning his 'sh's.' He might have been exchanging confidences with a drunken baby. Now he turned to us again, benevolently ferocious. 'Never been sold a pup, always been up too early,' his finger wagged. 'Always on his toes—that's me. Maybe I'm in the artistic way now, but it wasn't always like that. Got there by selling. Started selling as a young man. Sell anything. Why, I've been in pavement lights one time. Heavenly Pavement Lights they called 'em. Then there was Rudge's Cracknels, lovely cracknels they were too. And I sold additives.'

'Additives?' asked Martie, eyes wide.

'In a manner of speaking.'

Through that frame of french window those two were still at it. Harry spoke most; Eve seemed now to laugh, now to shake her head impatiently, then to break into a long sentence while Harry watched her gravely. A strange sunset coloured them, the early autumn sky was casting what seemed a green light, the garden was fused with green and yellow light so that things began to shine from themselves—michaelmas daisies made bright mauve lights, a brown brick glowed orange. There was a transparency in the air, a stillness of stained glass.

Mr. Barnett was explaining additives, how once he sold a motor-oil—and how one of his jobs was window-dressing garages at Christmas.

'On the road,' he was saying, 'you got to work quick. I was on my toes. That Xmas I'm making snowmen. Snowmen I'm making. Cotton-wool and top-ats and the rest. Now there you are—Cadell my mate e makes a snowman a day. Makes is snowman and knocks off. That's enough for Cadell. But not for yours truly, not a bit. Know what I do? I make a snowman every hour. One blooming hour and there's your snowman! And then I'm off in the van to me next snowman. Course, I carry them toppers with me. . . .'

Eve had come striding in, she grabbed hold of my arm:

'Please come into the garden a moment! Harry's got some damn-fool nonsense. Come on.' And out we went towards Harry, leaving Mr. Barnett a moment silenced, mouth open like an affable red toad, before I suppose beginning to rumble on again to Martie.

Eve made no bones about it:

'Now I don't know what this is all about,' she almost shouted. 'I say I'm going to a funeral, Harry says there's no funeral. He says no funeral exists. Yet I'm going to one tomorrow. See? Furthermore he says it's a story of mine. Furthermore he says a lot I say is stories. For instance the latest is I told stories about the riviera. What is this story business? Did I tell you "stories" about the riviera? You should know.'

Harry made a tired gesture. 'God, Eve, he does know too. He knows none of this fancy stuff you make up about things is true at all.'

'Well,' Eve turned to me. 'Well My Lord Judge? You see? Nothing I say is true.'

I pretended to be surprised. This was difficult, Harry knowing I knew: 'I don't quite see . . .'

'Heavens alive—didn't I tell you once about a summer I spent in the south of—of Italy? Didn't I *tell* you?'

It seemed that if she had told me, that made it right. The telling was the test.

'Yes, Eve, you did tell me I think. . . .'

She looked triumphant. She smiled at Harry: 'There you are!' she said, solving all.

Harry fidgeted with his foot. In that pause the sun fell lower, the sky really was green, the windows reflected a dull gold. A stillness abounded, things sparkled like dew in the shadows, night seemed to be rising from the earth.

And then Harry, the words drawn in pain from him, said slowly: 'Eve, I know about your family, your country home.' He paused and added miserably: 'In Burnt Oak.'

Eve said nothing. She only stared at him as though she could never believe this, her eyes seemed to peer all over his face as if she were looking for some real blemish. She just said: 'Oh.'

'I had to be sure. I found the address and I went there.'

She tried to make her smile hard, but it was tired: 'You're very clever.'

Harry went on in a dead voice: 'You'd better know everything. We know about yesterday too, you didn't go into that house. We waited for you.'

Eve pointed at me, her arm stretched out and her voice rose: 'Where exactly does *he* come into this?'

'I had to confide in someone. I had to have help. Don't you see what this is doing to me?'

She was trying to control herself. She tried to sneer: 'Spying? That's nice.'

'Oh and a hundred other things. Eve, *Eve*—that diary! You wrote it all up, I saw the thing when it was empty.'

Now she laughed: '*That?* Heavens, can't you see that was simply a game? It's the kind of thing anyone would do. Just a silly game. You surely can't . . . no, that's too much.' She went on laughing, suddenly sure again, everything excused and Harry in the wrong.

But he was in some kind of despair, he was determined. 'Please Eve, do understand—that's only one thing. There are hundreds of others. You're driving me insane with this—' And he went on slowly, definitely enumerating instance after instance. She stood there watching him, now saying nothing. She seemed to droop. She looked a child again. Again the child found-out—and I am not sure she did not make some attempt to enhance this, she pressed her lips smaller into a pursed O shape, she moved a foot about anxiously.

Harry went on for a long time. I stood on the dewing turf most awkward—very much of a third figure standing there. And as in such distraught moments the brain wheels off to find concern with something, anything else—and sees this something else all the more clearly—I watched with wonder that curious green twilight deepening, making its odd transparent tapestry of the stillness, making things shine yet weaving an unusual quiet as distinct as stitchwork, bright yet dusted gold. Once Peter walked out from the french windows, shivered there poised and heraldic, and as suddenly turned and disappeared.

Now and then a chord came over the air from the piano, Barnett was playing some song from an early musical comedy, evocative music of flannel-dance days. I noticed a queer smile come over Eve's face, I thought at first it would be the music—but she was too young for that. It was a curious reflective smile, the smile of someone seeing again old and loved toys. It had love in it. And I knew suddenly what a tenderness lay in the dreamlife that Harry was tearing up—they were dreams, not lies.

But he saw her smile too, he misunderstood it, he must have thought it some new mockery, for he suddenly burst out: 'God, Eve—I can't believe in you any more at all! I can't even believe about Erik! I don't believe there ever was an Erik, an aeroplane, a crash. . . .'

Eve stamped her foot and shouted: 'Shut up! Shut up about that!' There was a sob in her voice.

He stopped and looked frightened. She went on shouting: 'Shut up, shut up—leave that dead boy alone. . . .'

I remember taking a step forward. Whatever was at stake, Harry seemed abruptly a bully with her standing there sobbing and hurt.

Then as Harry began to stutter that he was sorry a voice came heartily just beside us: 'Now you three, what's this, kiss in the ring?'

Words like that fall on the air with a fearful momentary significance; and Martie had a genius for discovering them. We all turned and looked at her amazed. There she stood, beaming, announcing herself with unrestrained joy. 'Can't I play too?' Then she saw Eve wiping at the tears round her eyes and thought she had been laughing: 'My,' she said, '*that* must have been a good one!'

And Barnett had come up too. Always ready for a joke he made a comedian's grimace: 'Lumme—if your poor uncle were alive to hear that, it'd kill him!'

Both stood there laughing, they rocked there strangely —it was like seeing two sudden drunks, though this they certainly were not. And slowly, like some heavy machine beginning, we other three pretended a faint, unlovely chuckle.

There was nothing to do about it. We could not go on in front of them. Whatever Harry felt, he would not have a scene: he was too reserved, and his guests were both too much strangers. Eve followed his lead, patting herself together. We all turned and went inside to supper.

A depressed meal, a meal heavy with voices and heavier silences. We seemed more to eat the furniture that crowded round us than the meat on our plates. Neither Martie nor Mr. Barnett could have known that there had been that quarrel. We were of course over-polite to each other: so that two people reached for the salt at once—with a laughing clash that as suddenly subsided; so that second helpings were too formidably pressed; so that the beer was frequent but did nothing to intoxicate.

And the stippled, stone-coloured wallpaper closed coldly in. On the polished sideboard more trophies of engineering glimmered their steel diligence—an ashtray made from half a model sea-mine, a paper-knife like a propeller blade, a ship's derrick from which hung a silvery pencil on a silvery chain over a morocco telephone pad. On the walls, watercolours of Italian lakes dried their pale eyes. And Audrey, who had not moved the whole evening, now chose to sit up begging behind Martie's chair, grim and silent, like a small white unnoticed footman.

During one of the longer silences towards the end of that meal, Martie must have suspected that the matter of Eve's funeral might still hang on the air. She looked out at the weather—now clouded and dark —and murmured: 'I hope it'll clear up for your—for you tomorrow.'

Harry looked puzzled. But Eve said without a tremor: 'For the funeral? Yes . . . anyway it seems so often to drizzle at funerals.'

She turned to Harry: 'By the way, will you be needing the car? You know, I *am* going over there tomorrow.'

She said this levelly. She was firm. Harry looked down at his plate.

He muttered: 'I'll drive you over myself.' Then he looked at me quickly. 'You'll stay, won't you?'

He was pleading. I had to say I would. It was unbelievable—I was convinced there was no funeral. Apparently whatever had been discovered of her past had no connection with the future. And now I too was somehow involved, and I was genuinely saddened by the whole affair.

Later we put Barnett on the London train. He had bought the sad lifeless puppy—which I thought was nice of him, obviously he liked the livelier one but his sentiment chose to protect the little sad one—and I went up into a cheerless, most comfortable bedroom hung with more pale watercolours.

There was no argument on the following day. Eve looked pale and quiet; but it was difficult to tell whether this was a reaction or whether it was the beginning of the funeral. Harry said nothing further to me, nor I to him.

But we went to the funeral. Eve wore no black. She buttoned a raincoat round her and wore a mannish hat. It did not rain. But it was a desolate day, clouded and windless, soaked with a white wetness that never fell.

We stood and watched with a small scattered group

of mourners while the coffin was brought to the moist yellow clay, yellow as varnished pitchpine; while the pall-bearers in patched and old dark suits lumbered it forward, as though they wished to hurry it, while the coffin for some terrible reason of its own seemed to hold back: while the bright green artificial grass matting was rolled out near the hole. Who the dead person was we never knew: the dead go into the ground without names. Eve might have known: she might have seen an announcement in the paper.

At one moment one of the mourners came over to her and whispered. She flushed, Harry could not bear it, he quickly took her arm and nodding to the man gravely silenced whatever he had been about to ask. Once an elderly woman, pale and quiet, yellow clay on her black boots, walked a step forward to the grave and, as if perplexed, peered in. Could it be true? Down there?

A moment later I looked round to see Eve, still on Harry's arm, silently crying. I never knew whether she was weeping for this cold parade of death, or for Harry and herself. In her raincoat her shoulders shook.

IX

AFTER that I did not see them for many months.
I do not know whether this was the result of my
own fear of becoming further involved: or whether
it was a diffidence on Harry's part after revealing so
much. In any case—he was married now and he lived
outside London. Nor had it ever been very necessary
to meet, we were such old friends and so far apart that
time did not press us.

Only once he rang up. It was to ask me to spend a
weekend. We exchanged our usual consternation that
we never met nowadays, and why didn't we? Then I
said that alas I was too busy just then, and this was
partly true. I went on to ask him 'how things were?'
I must have said this less casually than I intended; for
he echoed, puzzled, the word 'things?' I reminded
him. He laughed: 'Oh *that*.' 'That' was all over and
forgotten long ago. He had worked out his attitude
towards 'that'. And I presumed that Eve had settled
down, with a more real responsibility, to life. That
evening at Oxley had had its effect.

Then months later—in early July—Harry telephoned
again. He suggested brightly that we made good
our holiday resolution of the year before. 'Madam
now has her passport,' he laughed.

I hedged with myself a little—I knew quite well that
Harry had asked me mostly to make use of me, as old
friends do. That is one of the great comforts of old
friends—with them one can follow one's own interests,
one can do almost anything without apologizing. In

E   121

this case I would be a useful guide. So I simply thought that I would make use of him back. My position stood as before—it was convenient to go away with a married couple, it would solve problems of loneliness and yet I could always escape without apology.

The outcome was that I agreed. And three weeks later we found ourselves humming down the Route Nationale. Past Lyons, past that point where the northern cloudbank edges the wide meridional sky as a grey carpet fits a blue. Humming—to the oilquiet speed of wheels, with the wind in our faces, to the thrum of trees flying backwards, with the road ever-opening forwards to a sun without end. Once more the prospect beckoned, once more the magic was on. However many times tired and a little less illusioned one returned—this prospect remained fresh, there was always this magic of return. It had been a rainy summer in England.

Eve was delicious. From the moment she set foot on French soil she became younger, prettier, livelier. She became radiant. She was like a pretty animal relaxing from the stealths of reality into play. Only, of course, Eve was relaxing from play into reality. She had never been abroad before.

She fell in love with the dingiest café tables, seeing heaven knows what gallic sins and gaiety in their diurnal void. She was charmed by old men with beards—never dreaming of the accountant's office, seeing only the grand old boulevardier. The French words frothed round her, she felt them to be wit—never prices. But perhaps I exaggerate, perhaps she was responding as much to the simple differences of shape and smell and sound that charmed us all.

We passed an excited English night in Paris, a happy hangover at Roanne, and on into the blue. We turned off through Aix, sniffed the dry graces of Provence, passed away from the shadow of Spain to where an Italian rigolo plays above the blue sonorities of France. We touched into Nice, and then turned back along the coast to a small place past Cannes. There they pleaded to settle, and we took rooms. And it was there, on the terrace of our hideous stippled red hotel, and facing a countryside of pines and sandy underscrub more like Surrey than Surrey itself, that one morning Eve yawned her arms out towards the sun, and sighed to me—we were alone—with surprising candour:

'You know—I've never been abroad before.'

Until then she had never stated this. Not, at least, to me.

'I expect you knew that though. After we had it out that evening at Oxley. Remember?'

I nodded, and made a deprecatory noise. And thanked the sun for giving me dark glasses.

'I can talk about it now,' she said, 'now that I'm really here. And you know—I was so sorry about all that passport business. What a fool!'

She turned to me with a shy look. 'Do you know why I did that?'

I fiddled with my coffee cup. I had finished it ten minutes before.

'No?'

'I was frightened.'

I smiled and looked shocked. 'But you're not frightened of *Harry* . . .?'

She made a small impatience of her hand. Then laughed lazily at me, at herself hot in the sun.

'No no. It wasn't Harry. Lord no. It was simply fright. You'll never believe me. Just fright. I was frightened of setting foot out of England. You can't understand that, can you? You're used to it. You wouldn't understand what it means to *risk* leaving home?'

I said that surely she was exaggerating.

'Well I'm not. I know I wasn't going alone and that you and Harry were there to look after me. But still ... it didn't feel safe, it frightened me. I don't know what I thought, I didn't think anything exact—just a jumble like 'foreigners' and 'what if I got lost' and all the dreadful tales they tell ...'

She looked at me shyly again.

'You're laughing—but it felt such a long way off. I haven't got a clear sense of places. It was safe at home —and you knew about the aunt I lived with in Burnt Oak? Well, once I had a hard struggle getting away from her—leaving home and all that. But I knew I could always rely on her—if I was in trouble. I don't think I wanted to get too far away from her, from my bolt-hole.'

She was speaking slowly, thinking down at her brown hands. I thought: 'Yes, there are still people like this.' And jokingly:

'So you led us up the garden path. Right until the last few days. Why did you leave it so late?'

'I got doubly frightened. I got frightened of—oh, explaining.'

'You cooked up a beautiful story, I must say.'

She bit her lip: 'You shouldn't—' she began, then softened and shrugged her hands. 'I had to.'

'But you needn't have really—we're friends and so on.'

'I know.'

She was silent, thinking. The waiter came and I ordered more coffee. She refused, half-there. Then:

'When I was younger I used to steal things. Not much, just pilfering. Just when I was hard up. I had plenty of friends I could borrow from. But I never did. It was easier to steal. That's what it was—*easier*. I didn't have to go through all that talk—explaining, troubling people, perhaps getting refused. Or reproached. Oh, those looks of reproach!

'If I'd owned up about that passport there'd have been reproach. However nice you were about it. That's what I feared. I don't think I ever like to throw myself on someone else's mercy.

'Yet it's not the mercy I mind so much—it's all that damned talk.'

She sighed and shook her head. Then she began to smile—it was the same distant smile I had seen that evening on the Oxley lawn when those dreams of hers were torn up. A smile almost of self-indulgence, of tender self-recollection.

So that was explained. And a little later, while we still sat lazing at the parasolled table, Harry came down. He wore only a pair of bathing-drawers. They were rather longer than those usually worn by the French along the coast—he managed still to look like an advertisement for an overcoat: perhaps a light-weight summer coat. His eyes twinkled above the clipped moustache. He was exuberant, he had found that there were tennis courts quite handy. I remember that morning well—I think because I was smugly pleased that Eve had so confided in me: and that she had been telling me, with reflective amusement, the truth.

Then we went down to bathe in the blue warm water. The little bay curved out on either side; our red modern hotel, with its liner windows and its sundecks, stood exactly in the centre. Just there the beach was littered with canoes of many kinds, with rubber floats and white-painted pedal-boats. There was always a shouting from the handball net. A group of Englishmen, pants hanging like dishcloth below their new short shorts, had set up some cricket stumps. People lounged everywhere on boards, and others came to sell them ices and drinks. And the two pine-heathery capes mothered round this hive of holiday. It was not very pleasant: but the warmth, the blue dancing water, the enlivening sun, the whole benevolence of a clear beautiful morning shed a tolerance on everything. Of all the mornings we bathed on that beach, it is of that one I retain the clearest photograph. Perhaps because nothing then had yet happened— though a sharp event was already assembling itself like a cloud upon a date in the following week. Or perhaps because by then none of the southern maladies had set in. But I think mostly because I was feeling smug and satisfied with my deduction of Eve. And glad that she had given up her story-telling.

However—in that again I was wrong. All moments of success are suspect. The moment one achieves a clear all-seeing idea is the moment to begin to be suspicious. But of course the last thing one does is to suspect. Brilliantly the pieces in the problem come together! Brilliantly the mind sees all! But at the very moment when the pieces approach their assembly, as the anthem of self-praise swells—one's own guard is going down, cautions are fading, defences thrown to the glad winds, and the puzzle is solved with only half a mind. One forgets that the pieces were never, in the first place, meant to come together at all.

Just so—a couple of days later I was alone in the garage café with Harry and I took it upon myself to say how glad I was that Eve had 'grown up.'

He just laughed.

'I don't know about that,' he said. 'Though it's nice of you to think of saying it. It'd be more true to say that *I'd* grown up.'

I asked him what he meant. He was quite at ease, he had said that very happily. It was hot, we sat in the shade by the petrol pumps, and petrol and a smell of fruit mingled busily with the taste of drinks, the noise of huge lorries, and the sense of hot white dust in the sun all around.

'I had a bad time working it out,' he told me, 'after I saw you last. After that funeral. Of course the little blowing up I gave her did its good. But there was still the funeral—that was one gun she was sticking to. It meant she hadn't given it. She knew she couldn't be found out about it. So I knew there'd be other events like it. There were.

'I thought I'd go mad, old man. It got worse, it was awful. At last I made an excuse and went away for a few days.

'And God I'm glad I did. For only doing that showed me, suddenly, very plainly, what course I should take. It wasn't any thinking out that I did—it was the very fact of going away. Because, you know . . . I—I found out I was so lonely without her, I found out I loved her so much above all other things. It just came clear that my love for her, and that only, was what mattered. Whatever else happened came second, what came first was I loved her. I loved her more than anything else in the world . . . I know that's an old saying—but because I was actually *doing* it I could see how clearly it did mean really "anything else in the world". She might murder, rob, poison, do anything —I'd still love her. All those silly stories, those innocent daydreams meant nothing. I had to pinch myself and wonder whether *I* had been dreaming—making so much of it!

'After I saw that it was all right. Everything was all right. I took no decision, it was nothing like that. It was more as you say—like growing up.

'I went back. The first thing she greeted me with when I got there was—another story! An obvious one, plain out in the daylight—and you know how bad at it she can be, going on and on adding details till she's forgotten what she said first. And do you know what?—I found I wanted just to laugh! I wanted to laugh and take her in my arms! But of course I didn't—oh no! I sat there listening—watching her and loving her for it! She looked so like a child playing! I suppose I had a sort of twinkle in my eye—and as a matter of fact that twinkling feeling's the only thing that I feel dubious about now— it's far too superior, it feels too damned daddy-wise.

'So there you are. On she goes—perhaps not quite so much as before, and she's rather more careful—and I listen. And we're happy as . . . as . . .'

What he was happy as was lost, for just then a giant trailer-lorry roared by carrying its burden to Toulon. But whatever it was, he looked it. He was neither hesitating nor understanding. And I remember wondering again at so much confession from a reserved type of man, wondering again at this curious privileged position of mine: of the years.

As confessor, I did not so easily know what to say. But when the lorry had passed: 'I'm very glad to hear it, Harry . . . But I must say she's—I mean Eve's not said anything much out of the ordinary lately—to me at least. . . .'

'She's wild about all this: she's too taken up—she's living for once instead of dreaming.'

He waved his hand vaguely round the place—inconsequently indicating no more than petrol pumps, dust, oildrums and a priest cycling by. But I knew what he meant. And I nodded. Then I remembered with a light irritation the reversal of my own deductions. And I began telling him how she had told me the story behind the story of the lens smugglers and that old passport business. I told him—at dangerous length— what she had said about being frightened. 'Now is that,' I asked him straight, 'the truth or a story?'

He took a sip of his drink, considered a moment, then said: 'I should think—the truth. Yes, truth. She told me the same, of course.'

Then he smiled.

'But you're tripping me. What does it matter if it *is* the truth or not? In the end—I don't really know that it is, and I'm damned if I care.'

Then he added: 'What is the truth anyway? You bloody highbrows are always beefing about Truth in your books. What *is* this Truth?'

That I was not letting myself in for.

'I don't know,' I said, edging off. 'But I don't think it has much to do with lies.'

That finished that, and soon an olive-skinned young

god dark with motor-grease came to tell us the car was serviced: and we drove back to lunch.

During the next three days nothing unusual occurred. We led the life of the little plage, and scarcely left it. It was very hot, no sign of a mistral blowing up for some time. It was relaxing outside the water, and except in the evening nearly oppressive. Sweat dripped down blinding the eyes. Sunglasses slipped about in the sweaty hair round the ears and had constantly to be polished. Even in the shade one stuck to things—to one's shirt, to a wickerwork chair. For coolness, for escape, one drank too many iced aperitifs.

Very quickly the naked bodies about became ordinary. There were several very beautiful girls, and some fine-bodied men—at first these took one's breath away and provoked self-comparisons better left quiet. But soon, with familiarity, even the best flesh could be criticized. It could be seen to wobble too much here, to cave in or to bulge too much there. New and old boil-marks were discovered, and people wore on the tough rubber of brown skins a variety of purple and pale green bruises—one imagined that somewhere in the night there walked abroad a prurience that came up behind the ladies and pinched them with fingers stained in billiards-chalk and mauve wine.

However—to revive one's sense of the beauty of these people there was a short and easy cut—one had only to swivel one's sweat-smeared eyes across the planks and the gritty sand to a group of northerners. And there was flesh for you! The finest white squid-flesh cankering from the most ill-fitting playsuits! Gin-weaned women of thirty, faces pocked with bad cosmetics, strutted their veined legs in rompers designed for children of ten. Crab-red men lay burning sore, their flaccid arms like neon-tubes, their heads shameless in great blue peaked caps. How they scampered, how they cried—and what bundles they carried with them! Clobbery great beach-bags, virulent scarves, clinical towels, a hundred shoes and an agony of little cameras! And—but look back at the brown-skinned again, the naturally elegant, and for some minutes again there is beauty.

The malaises of the south set in—climatic diarrhoea, queer rashes and pink-eye, the itch of over-eating and the cafard that too much pernod leaves behind. Large and fearful mosquitoes zoomed their warning on the evening air—but these were nothing to the slow-flying small ones, elfin and delicate, quiet and nearly invisible, which floated and stung, stung, stung. No warning, no pic, no sight of these. . . . And in the day pale flies bit one on the sand. To all these discomforts there was only one answer—to drink more. And that answer was a spiral, a vice-loving hot spiral.

One morning we walked along the beach to bathe quietly and alone off the rocks. We walked right along to the end of the cape, passing new plasterette villas grinning between the pines—and no architecture has less dignity than those torrid little film-sets of the south —to where rocks straggled out into the water. There the water ceased to be blue, it became purple and green, and it was wonderfully clear. Harry and myself soon had the black oursin needles in our toes, painful and quick to fester: and Eve was sucked at by a small, malevolent, pale brown octopus. We tried to sunbathe on the rocks, finding flat places: but none were flat enough, or big enough, and in a few minutes one ached from the hard stone. So we went back and sat down on the baking grit. Later some boys came along with harpoons and goggled masks. They swam out, and soon came back with Eve's octopus, or a liver-coloured one like it, hung like a wet rag on the trident. They took it up near us, banged it down on the beach: like a wet wakening spider it curled out its arms and began instinctively to walk seawards: its head stuck up absurdly, goggling and wobbling, as it prised its way along. The boys picked it up again, banged it down; then one of them stuffed his hand inside and thus, while it was still living, still wreathing its long suckers round his arm, pulled its stomach inside out. It lay there bluish white blubber, dead. We went back to the hotel.

In the afternoons, despite the heat, Harry used to go up to the village behind and play tennis. He had a hard holiday energy, and he sweated through the gruelling afternoon heat. He derived both pleasure and virtue from this. I made one or two excursions about the neighbouring countryside—trying at first to walk, then hiring one of those ridiculous but really slow and pleasant bicycles that have a small motor attached instead of pedals. At some facetious moment this was labelled 'The Vicar's Daughter'—a sort of family joke, though sounding more like an instrument of mediaeval torture—but it was really most comfortable. However, I rode her less and less: and more and more took a siesta—and this, though hot and sleepless, was the most precious moment of the daylight. It was quiet then; the shutters were closed, a grey light dusked the room, bright chinks of sunlight showed the glare so happily exiled. The ancient blue sky roared away motionless and deep somewhere outside: and inside the cool pillow, where I lay loving it and yet regretting that I too did not play tennis. Though I indulge the other animal senses, I miss altogether that beautiful and necessary instinct for leaping the body about: games are organized, and for this I have a solitary's dislike, I am condemned not to bend or twist my body. So I laid myself down instead: and worked a little, and read, and tried to sleep. Because of this, after the siesta, and while Harry still played tennis, I saw quite a lot of Eve alone.

She was still charmed with all she saw. With her brushed blonde hair and her brown skin, in her shorts tight-framing so well the long plump smooth brown legs, even in the formidable black and gold glasses that made a beetle of her eyes—she looked charming. And she was charmed. Though now, in retrospect, I know there was something she found lacking. I remember now—though I paid no attention to it at the time—how she used to stare for a long while at one of the old and spacious villas that remained in that new-built settlement. It was a square yellow villa of the turn of the century, it had tall shutters, a flamboyance of pillar and pediment and encaustic tile; and there was a garden of palms and yucca and oleander nurturing a luxuriant, rich calm. Its terrace was balustraded, its darkness looked cool and tile-floored within. Eve used to look long at this, and then sigh. I thought at the time that this was a sigh of pleasure, but looking back I see it was very much a sigh of displeasure.

And once or twice, I remember, I found her sitting gazing about her less enchanted than puzzled. Something, in fact, beyond all the novelty, was lacking. Something was not living up to the picture she had drawn in her mind. I do not think she objected to the beach-machines and the villas, nor the neat Surrey aspects. No, she was not criticizing what was there: she was wondering instead what was not there. I was soon to know the nature of this.

And once, though I thought at the time she was content, I did receive a startling, and saddening, shock. It was in the evening, after dinner, when we were sitting out on the terrace and enjoying the moonlit sea and the cooling air. The moon scattered its gold to the horizon, and the sea to either side was varnished black. There was a smell of night-trees, and all that during the day might have offended the eye was embalmed in a different light. It was as if a warm snow had fallen, whitening surfaces not seen before, throwing others into deep silent shadow. Overhead, the great stardust. And down on the beach pedal-boats were ranged like weird-boned monsters of the moon; and along the coastal motor-road occasional headlights cast tall moving shapes on the hillside like the sails of ghostly feluccas; away to sea the lights of boats and of villas on the cape played their astounding dancing game. At our table we tasted this flowering of the evening air, the coolness of fresh linen, the comfortable glasses of brandy, the comfort of fine food eaten.

I noticed that Eve had her diary out, and she was bent over it scratching hard with a stub of pencil. She bent close, licking the pencil and jabbing it hard at the diary. I saw she was not writing but crossing something out, harshly, over and over again. I watched her, so absorbed, for a while: then murmured that indeed it must have been an unpleasant error to deserve such emphatic treatment. She looked up, smiled wrily, and propped the book up for me to see.

It was the first page, the page giving all dates of the year. And each day of the year so far had been blacked out by a hard black square. There was vehemence in this erasure. And where months were completed thick lines had scored them out with vigorous relief—another month passed! I saw that the days of our holiday had been as passionately blacked out as the days in England.

I looked at Eve in sudden surprise. Brown, healthy, young, beautiful, newly married. Why such a deep black wish for the days to pass?

'You seem to be in a hurry to get it over,' I said.

She looked at the marks negligently, as at a game: 'Oh, I've always done that.'

A game! I saw that the very date of that day had been started before its time. And suddenly I remembered how, when I was much younger, I used to look forward in the winter to summer; and then as soon as the summer came, how I counted the days until Christmas. I was impatient for the future, greedily and nervously impatient. Something wonderful might, *would* happen! The present, for no good reason, did not satisfy. An eagerness to be getting on with it—and I do not know whether that meant getting towards some miracle ambition or getting life over with altogether. But whatever the deeper implications, it was an unhappy state. It meant plainly that life as it stood was lacking.

So life could not be living up to Eve. However, she made nothing of it—no deep sighs on the warm night air: she snapped the book to, unmoved by it, and began pleasantly to talk of other things.

X

ON the great corniches of the French Riviera there
is an occasion that has come to be called 'le pile-
up anglais.' With the changes in currency of the times,
it may now have become ' le pile-up americain': or
'suédois'. But in any case it is essentially a 'pile-up
nordique'—that is the root point.

These great cliff motor-roads are finely accomplished
works of engineering—their smooth grey surfaces slide
a clean and beautiful cordon along the mountain edge,
the stone emplacements that side and support them are
built like fortress walls, and for the eye their curving
and bending presents always a new and surprising
vista round buttresses, through tunnels, or up to the
mountains—where sometimes the three roads can be
seen like a chord of pale worms against the great
earth—or down to the sea where a hair-pin bend reveals
some new blue harbour inkling below.

But the finest engineering cannot take into account
the Great White Northern Spirit Belt. And in the
tourist months these roads stream with the long cars
of pale-eyed northerners accustomed not to the slow
southern wines but to fiercer liquors of their own cold
homes. These visitors turn the hour of the aperitif into
a high gin fling, a muzz of schnapps and cocktails. They
are fooled by the long leisurely hours at café tables:
unaccustomed to sip, accustomed to drink quickly in
the more restricted minutes of their north, unused even
to the space about them—a space that at moments can
seem to merge at last with time—they gulp their

drinks at a nervous speed: they are fooled too by the aperitifs themselves, to whose slow intoxication they add little lacings of white spirit; and they do not understand the strange powers of pastis. So with so much sun and so much sense of well-being they are often too wild soused to drive by the time of a late lunch or dinner.

The peak hours for the pile-up, the hours when these roads become really dangerous, are between one and two o'clock at mid-day and seven and nine o'clock at night. Never take your loved ones driving then. There may indeed be trouble at other times, there are the long shots, there are the headlights of the night, there are the hit-or-miss five-o'clocks. But those two are the peak hours.

Knowing this, but ourselves too fortified with liquor to mind, Eve and Harry and I took to the corniche one evening at sometime about sunset.

We had driven into Cannes for the day. We had wandered about in hot offices changing money, in Eve's parfumerie shadowy with scent and cool with pale attendants, in various bars and cafés and along the palmed promenade and hot harbour quay. We had eaten a magnificent and expensive lunch, we had muttered to ourselves that Cannes was a sea of orange masts. Though one might not have wished to live there, it looked in all rather magnificent. The holiday machine at highest gear. Over-size, over-glitter. Huge hotels whiter than elsewhere, yachts larger than in other harbours. One walked the quays and looked down at wealthy yachtsmen eating their meals like captive bears in polished wood pits; one strolled over the packed bronze bodies on the beach and marvelled at flesh stretching far beyond eyes' reach. The air was golden with the drip-drip-drip of money.

Then we took the road back. Harry did not drive fast. There was a lot of traffic on the road, and a westering sun blazed sometimes head-on into the eyes: then one could see nothing, one simply hoped. Immense lorries abruptly loomed, leaving as suddenly nothing but a black smoke. We were passed by monstrous sleek roadsters driving at speed to the day of their own pile-up. The road snaked and sped, we passed idyllic coves of rock sunset red against mauve water and great white square hotels covered with plastic lettering. The mountains took us in their lovely ascent, and once we drove across the estuary of a dry river. We held our breaths as three cars came suddenly head on round a precipitous bend, we gasped as a fleet of bicycles rose from the road like phantom skittles. We passed one pile-up with its dead-slumped radiator and its ragged little crowd. And then at last we rounded the last cape home, we saw the mast of our hotel among the pines and breathed a sigh of home-blown relief.

Then we got ours.

It happened from nothing in a second, the second then lasted at leisure. A car blinding round rock towards us, another from behind trying to pass at speed, Harry twisting off the road to where the stump of a fat cork-tree awaited us.

But at the time it was all only a sudden cyclone of shapes whirled up nowhere, from smooth passage a great looming of mass and shape, a lurching of sudden ships, a roof one way, a bonnet the other. Horn roar —one chorded blast above tyres whipped screeching, skid of brakes—and then as the brain caught what was happening, the slow leisurely commencement of the journey to the cork-tree, aerial and pleasant.

Clear, clear it became—there was time for sound and touch and sight to divide and lay themselves out separate for inspection. As for a matter of twenty feet we raced at speed to the cork-tree, there seemed time to take everyone's number, light a cigarette, look around. Time ballooned, we seemed to float in the balloon, the big extraordinary slow bubble drifting towards what the mind still well knew to be hard and fearful impact. I remember the ring round a tree where the cork had been sliced off, and that once Eve had told me wonderingly when she first saw this that she had always believed cork came from the sea. Then there was the dashboard, static and glittering with figures and silver. And an ashtray, stuffed up with cigarette stubs. And then the mind had time even to rationalize, to see in its aerial drift glass all around, and slowly to bow the head and cover with hands the eyes.

Thus in golden slow weather we crashed nose-on into the fat hard tree. Instant blackness, time so slow speeded up enormously into blackness. Into blackness that threw my head what felt upside down, so that suddenly through the blackness as through a window I was looking up straight into the open sky and seeing, definitively paused in mid-air, the sailing shape of a pair of sunglasses. They looked like a winged creature, an insect-cupid all eyes. They marked the stop. The stop to which everything had whirred at phantasmal speed up. The high, the short momentous stop. Then . . . the spectacles moved on, drifted out of sight, and the great thudding sound of our crash came as time sighed sobbing down to usual measure.

I saw their two stunned faces in the front seat moving round at each other and then to me—like two people waking up in a double bed and looking round to the clock which was me. They looked at each other, they mumbled 'All right?', they sighed 'Yes'; then still stupefied they looked round to see what the time was by me. It was plainly shockingly late. Their faces screwed up with horror—and then instead of gasping the time they gasped my name. Then: 'God, your face!'

They looked sick. I remembered slowly putting my hand up and feeling it warm and wet. I looked at my hand, and there was for a moment a pleasure in the red and wetness of the blood—before concern set in. I put my hand up again—and at the same time jutted my head down to look in the mirror. One side of my face and forehead was streaming red. I was horrified, I felt caged and fated. By then Eve had a handkerchief out and was wiping. Then she was saying: 'It's nothing, it's only a cut.'

I must have hit my forehead on something; but it never hurt, it was nothing. And then we all began—I suppose hysterically—to laugh.

Then doors opening; and with the return to life a sudden sense of capability, resolution of a thing well done. One was capable of surviving death, of looking after one's life. And as we rose carefully, and still with a certain astonishment, more senses seemed to come to work. There came smells of car-leather and petrol in the sun, the first smells for a long time: and small sounds—a distant boat-siren, in its far water ignorant of our catastrophe: and the busy throb of cicadas which must have sung before we arrived, as we crashed, and now still sang: and a sense of how extraordinarily still the country can be.

'Hell!' I said, looking at the astonishing mush of radiator and mudguard crumpled into the tree, 'hell, that was a narrow one.'

'Damn fools!' Harry swore. 'We'll see about this!' And he was walking away to where people were walking towards us. Then he called back to me a command: 'Here, come and interpret.'

Eve was standing and muttering, 'Where . . . where . . .?'

'You all right?' I said anxiously.

She looked at me, I think she was shocked and pale; she just said: 'I've lost my glasses.'

Then Harry and I were gabbling with the people from the car that had been coming towards us, and which had stopped some hundred metres further on. The car that had cut in had, as might have been expected, raced straight on and long ago vanished. Perhaps in the exhilaration of steering clear it never knew we had crashed: but perhaps it did, and feared much the worst.

We were on a curved stretch of road quite a way outside our village. On one side was this small cork plantation rising up to a ridge beyond which lay the sea: on the other side lay a big-leaved field of maize and away in the flat country a pink-tiled farmhouse. It was open country, the pines and the villas had not yet begun. Nevertheless a small crowd soon collected —two labouring men, an old lady, a vigorous motor-cyclist in white plus-fours and a leather jacket loose about his naked chest. We were on a main road, a grey smooth road that cut through the sunset country—and along this constantly came other cars. They slowed down, and looked curiously at us as they passed: they looked at the ground for blood, and sometimes laughed between themselves before they knew they would see none. Some stopped to ask if anyone needed help— but for every one that stopped, eight passed on.

Harry was angry. 'Christ, they might have killed her,' he said astonished when he knew the other car had gone on—and this was in his mind while everybody of that small crowd talked at once. Each had seen the pile-up, or imagined they had seen it. I had the impression that all that thicket and field innocent to either side had really been studded with heads camouflaged watching. As they gestured and the French spurted, so Harry controlled his anger—and the capable leader, the man of considered action, showed. He came into his own. The bones of his face set themselves patiently, his eyes looked from one to the other with considered penetration—and calmly he commanded, he stopped them all talking at once, he listened to one after the other. They stood, the voluble ones, waiting on his words. In his long khaki shorts he looked like a commander detailing subordinate officers in the field.

He listened only to what was relevant. And I translated—it was as ordered as that. And in a few moments he found that no-one had the number, or any detail, of the other car. It was only a large grey car. He saw that nothing was to be done. And as evenly as he had taken command, he dismissed himself—no use in blathering about—and stepped out into the road and stopped the next car. Would they kindly stop at the garage at the entrance of the village and send a break-down car? The driver, at first annoyed at being stopped, responded with charm. He asked even whether he could take Madame in to her hotel?

Harry looked at Eve and nodded.

'You go along,' he said.

She shook her head—she said nothing, but took his arm and simply stood there.

'Go on,' he said, 'you're knocked up.'

'No.'

So the car drove on. We went over and sat in a row on the mudguard: while our little crowd, left standing at ease, burst into chatter among themselves, reconstructing, gesturing, arguing. We sat silent, three abreast, watching them as if we were in a tram. Presently the owner of the cork-tree came up. He enquired whether anyone had been hurt—by this time I had wiped the blood from my face—and then began to wonder about his cork-tree, which was splintered and a little bent: visions of the mysteries of insurance must have presented a bank-note to his mind.

Thirsty we waited. Then the break-down crane like a red circus machine came jogging up, and we all helped hoist the shattered axle from its place of rest. I remembered the spectacles I had seen in the air, and took Eve to where they might have fallen. We searched, and found them glinting out in the open between those low bushes. They winked malevolently as lost things do—they had plainly been hiding in a fine place of their own and only now had scuttled out, crabwise, to reveal themselves.

At last we drove off, helpless in the car coupled to the break-down van. I remember feeling glad the car was thus for a while out of action—no more busy expeditions, no more discussion of performance and maps. But also, as we entered the streets, ashamed to be seen thus limping and powerless. It was ridiculous —as though one had slipped on a banana-skin.

The manager of the garage had come to drive us in, and now that same oil-smeared young god came to greet us. He threw up his hands in commiseration at the sight of so smashed a bonnet and was quick to uncouple the car. Then, while the manager went to attend to something, he showed a most kind concern for us— we must have suffered? So great a shock—and he brought from somewhere at the back a glass of wine. Which he gave to Eve. Madame must sit here, where it is comfortable, and drink this—it is cool. He stood looking at her, a fine vigorous olive figure—and I saw that he looked perhaps for just too long a time, and too vigorously, and that he was not so young, he was a man.

But perhaps I was simply irritated by having no wine myself; or by the enviable charm of such men. At least I remember feeling what a good thing a little money was—at least we could take Eve away from such potent figures to the sanctity of the hotel, at least that was some compensation for the striving that had lost so much middle-aged hair from the head . . . whereas, if the field had been even and open?

Unpleasant thoughts, both ways. But by then perhaps the aftermath of the accident had begun, the unwinding of alerted nerves. In any case, Eve had nothing herself to do but thank him, she was most concerned with her discovered sunglasses, and we left to walk back to the hotel.

That night at dinner the dullness set in more deeply. We were crestfallen and dully tired. I once heard somewhere a theory of the difference between a Latin and a Nordic reaction to a motor accident—say, a Frenchman's and an Englishman's. Naturally volatile, the Frenchman's nerves go up at the time; he passes through—and expresses—an immediate and intense play of emotions: when the danger is past, all subsides and he resumes a normal volatility. But in the English-man's case, an attack on the nerves intensifies his defences—what is called his normal of 'reserve': he tends to act coolly: he may thus seem at the time to take the accident the better in his stride—yet it is precisely this concentration of nervous defence that finds its complement later, for later there is nervous reaction, hours later comes the jangling and the upset.

That is one theory: and it did seem to apply to Harry and myself as we munched that evening through some rather large, and very bony, fish. Of course, the event was recapitulated at great length. Our slow English voices drawled out the thing in all its detail less to discover anything new than simply to speak, to make the mind think. Eve alone was very, very bright indeed.

She sparkled. She had plainly been stimulated rather than depressed. One had to wonder again at the strange ways of the mind. Normally, though certainly not unbalanced, she was in her way maladjusted. Her way was to live overmuch in the imagination. Yet for the imaginative, reality should be anticlimax? But again, reality often has the very opposite effect— it stimulates other dreams . . . and I wondered to myself what visions Eve had of herself lying torn and bloody by the roadside, or virgin again in her shroud in the cool farmhouse, or simply as a lonesome gravestone high in the classic winds of a Mediterranean hill.

XI

DURING the next days, as happens when death has been near and nicely averted, we resumed our lives with greater seriousness.

Harry threw himself with new energy into his afternoon tennis; and in the shade of the evening market place he spent more time watching the boule-game, of which he was making a study. We bathed less. It seemed a time for action. I began to write more up in my room, and absented myself with a notebook in the old port nearby and in the neighbouring countryside. I don't know that this effort added up to very much more work—but it seemed to. And Eve began to bustle about those many things that a woman finds to do—fitting herself out with more comfortable sandals, getting her hair done, visiting the chemist, buying notepaper and postcards and I don't know what else. Of course, there was another reason for all this. We had no car. The phantom of having a car had for a time disappeared. Although indeed we had not used it much, the idea of being able to use it and the vision of all the country within our grasp had thankfully been stolen from us: we were turned in upon the locality alone. Greater interest blossomed.

And now I must say something of the geography of the little place where we stayed. It will not take long. Regard our hotel—the only sizeable hotel—as the central point on a small strip of beach. Behind and to the east, a small land-village now become almost a township; it contained a few shops and cafés, a Place de la République formerly the Place of so-and-so and formerly so-and-so, which formed the plane-shaded sandy strip for boule-players and festal dances. And to the west of our hotel, where the beach ended and deep water drove a few yards in, there lay the still small and older sea-village, the fishing port with a few narrow alleys, a couple of cafés, and again a few shops. That is all. Further west and further east and into the hills extended the sub-tropical Surrey landscape, patched here and there with a palm and cactus garden, or with a field of Indian corn or vine. Thus—from west to east—the port, the hotel, the big village. One, two three. All interconnected with cottages and the villas of doctors and advocates.

In our new daily round Eve and Harry took a direction mostly towards the Place. Harry in the early evening for boules, Eve during the day for shops. I tended to go in the opposite direction—towards the port. In spite of so many so widely successful paintings, I still like a port. So it was quite natural that on the third or fourth day after our accident I happened to be botanizing in those narrow alleys.

It was the afternoon, latish, and life was beginning to stir again after the greatest heat. Movements behind the bead curtains of the cool butter-shop. A single whack from the butcher. A rearrangement of the last loaves in the bready shade of the baker. Two or three old women in black passed from the place where they had been mending nets to the slit backdoors of their homes—where, tireless old women, they would set about something else. A few children sat by doors making shell necklaces, idly, as though there would be something better to do later on. A fisherman in a blue cap hurried along to his slow boat.

There is really little difference in these paces of port life and the life in the little streets by the Place: what I think finally is the satisfaction to be got from ports is the sense of round shapes about—the rounder mouldings of stone, the curves of boats, the round of the harbour itself, the cylinder of lighthouse or bastion: roundness, if you like, that is womby; or, if you like, round as the ancient sun; or both, as you like. But round and satisfying.

That afternoon I found as usual much of interest. I found an arrangement of creeper-pots on a high window-sill, precarious and asymmetric, yet as still and green as the earth that did not exist in those stone alleys. I found in the clear harbour water a discarded pile of oursins of a type new to me—they were armed with curious and few very long spikes. I found an old boat-house far from the water, and saw how its ancient runway ended at the wall of a house built since. I found, as always, new and beautiful combinations of colours in the pigments washed on the walls. I found Eve with the young garage-man.

I had rounded the corner of a stone street of sharp sun and shadow—and there they were with their backs to me! They stood at the far end of the short street, I saw Eve first, I was about to call out, I thought she was just passing an unknown man in overalls. But as the sound rose to my lips they turned and laughed to each other, profile to profile, with a small strolling sway towards each other. They were undoubtedly together.

I backed round the corner again. Panic. Anger.

Then curiosity, dangerous compelling curiosity. I sauntered—there is no other word for it—round the corner. They were still there. They had stopped where they had laughed. They were still talking and laughing. I stood in the shadow—and so found myself, as at that time back by the Chelsea tea-shop, again watching Eve. I felt I should not do this; then I felt I should. Reasons for and against poured in and out. I hesitated —perhaps the smallness of the village, the slowness of life made this little sudden action too much of an event for me, I was a villager at the lace window. And while I still hesitated, the garage-man motioned with his arm, almost bowed Eve to a doorway to the left. He did not touch her. They disappeared into the doorway.

All my latent puritanisms rose like cold hellfire. But—what, after all, was this? Eve had been walking about, happened to pass the garage-man in this particular street, greeted him, asked him about the car? It happened to be the street where he lived? Or where friends lived—and he had simply asked her in to sit down a moment or see some curiosity or other? I imagined the dark little room full of laces and crucifixes and big old furniture—and above all old women sitting sewing, or stewing a pot with their great ladles. Nothing more natural. Then I remembered that the doorway belonged to a small dark cheap pleasant bar.

All right. Then the garage-man knew the proprietor of the bar. Or something. Anything.

But as I stood there wishing the best, I knew I had to know the worst. Yet—it was unthinkable to walk in and fabricate a surprised meeting. And in that climate of shade and sunshine, with the door of the bar naturally open, I could hardly get near enough to observe unobserved. In fact I could only wait there by the rough stone wall. What had been normally a street full of small interests grew blank—a wind of urgency blinded all good slow sight. Then it suddenly seemed absurd to stand there any longer. I walked back and away to the harbour behind.

I went over Eve's movements of the previous days. They could mean anything. Then I wondered what it mattered in any case—that is, in case she was seeing this garage-man regularly on the quiet. I had no pressing bond of loyalty to Harry. And I was not, I hoped, stupid enough to resent differences of class and nationality between Eve and that garage-man. But I was not above the ordinary male instinct to resent any other man intruding upon any woman—provided that man was not somehow of my own selection: an instinct not unlike the excited, purposeless barking of other male dogs round a bitch in rut.

A woman went down to the rocks by the small harbour mole with a cat curiously large for those parts, and the cat paddled with her in a rockpool. I hardly noticed this. I was too engaged. And in half an hour I was back again edging round that corner under the impression that now these two would have left the bar.

And indeed the bar was empty. It was so empty, so cool, so dark, so much without time that at once the whole town seemed empty. Even the proprietor was not there. Five feet of zinc counter, plain benches and marble tables, a large flyblown card detailing like a chart of railway freightage the law of drunkenness, the one colourful reredos of bottles. Nothing else but glazed yellow walls. Then there were noises in the back and in shuffled the proprietor. I ordered a pastis.

He was a big-moustached old chap, inelegant and abrupt. He wore an old khaki wool jacket over his collarless shirt, he served his drinks in a gruff business-like way, grunting to himself. I drank in silence and he sat himself to stare unsmoking at the beaded sunlit door. The silence continued. There I was—but I had no idea what I could ask this man. Simply to ask whether Mme. Camberley had been there was useless, I quite knew she had been. And I dared not throw out any hint—'Madame is gay to-day'—for fear the proprietor knew the garage-man and would smell a rat: and for fear in any case that any general questions would only lead to general answers and more general wondering. What, in fact, if Madame *was* gay? And so on.

I began to give it up and reached for my wallet—and this gave me at last an idea. A very simple idea. If *she* had paid, then the relationship was not necessarily intimate. If *he* had paid, then they knew each other well. Ideas breed more ideas; the next moment I was asking the proprietor:

'Monsieur, I wonder whether you would be good enough to change an English pound sterling?'

The old man's face showed no emotion, but his voice softened in apology:

'I regret indeed, Monsieur. But I cannot permit myself to make these exchanges.'

He gave no reason. He was not disposed to speak. Silence. The glass beads hung still as tubes in the sunlight. As in afterthought, I said:

'I'm so sorry. I thought it was you who had changed a note for my friend—the English lady who was here a few minutes ago?'

Again his face showed no surprise, but now he shifted his old grey slabs of eyes and fixed me with a disappointed stare:

'But Madame changed no note with me. Monsieur is mistaken.'

I mumbled that I must have been, and stared hard at the law of drunkenness as I paid. When suddenly the old man—it was almost as though the touch of money bribed him—said clearly and objectively:

'Besides, Madame did not pay. Naturally her companion paid.'

I left him staring at the bead curtains through which I hurried and I walked fast down and round the alleys. Now I had something! I was elated and excited and horrified.

Then I slowed down. For *what* had I found out? Doubts came in from everywhere. I found I had found out nothing. I had only been guilty of quick generalization—the kind that breeds a maxim. 'A woman in love etc.' or 'One does this because one does that.' Definitions of human habit that sound so immaculate, but whose exact opposite can later be seen equally to be true, whose only strength lies in the blinding acumen of words.

I had thought that if he paid, then she must be familiar with him. But what if she had offered to pay, and his pride—since only a small amount was involved—had revolted? Or what if she had held from paying, simply from fear of such pride—which he in fact had not? Or perhaps they had forgotten to pay—and as they walked out the proprietor had called 'Monsieur!' And then they had both struggled to pay, laughing at the game, and he had by chance won? Or perhaps she had slipped him a note under the table? Or boldly on the table? And so—on and on. I had learned nothing. I had only relearned the old lesson of our great human weakness for definition.

And later it occurred to me, with discomfort, that if that bar was by chance a usual meeting place for them —it was far from the Place, the tennis, and Harry— then according to his mood the proprietor might become suddenly eloquent, he might tell them all about the strange story of Madame's English friend and the pound note. And what would Eve think about that?

That night she was as gay as before; and the next day, when Harry complained that he really ought to go in and hurry up those mechanics, she very quickly interrupted him. She was going in to have her hair done, the hairdresser's was almost on the way to the garage—she could easily call in and save him the trouble. Anything not to get in the way of his old boules! And then—laughing—she said that in any case a woman would get more attention than a man— 'you know these French!' One cannot write that she said this without batting an eyelid, for in the nature of the remark she batted a great deal too many. And she batted very boldly.

When she came back that evening it was with the news that the car was ready, it could be picked up that night or the next morning. Harry was delighted, and immediately proposed an expedition. Eve was delighted. We sat in the evening cool sipping our aperitifs and discussing where to go. The shadows lengthened round the beach machines, suddenly the sun sank away, the machines disappeared and the night overwhelmed us with loveliness. Harry had heard of an old hill town with part of a ruined tower, some barren fortification against Saracen pirates. He twinkled at me, as though this concluded the matter: 'Just your kind of weather!' I nodded enthusiastically. I detest ruined towers. But it seemed a very good way of all getting together again—I nearly wrote, of keeping Eve off the streets.

So the next morning came—and we were dawdling the last of our breakfast. It was the moment when the bottom of the coffee cup is drained, when the last unread page of the paper is glanced through gluttonously, when pats are given to the pocket for the reassurance of cigarettes and money. Harry and I stood up. Eve remained sitting.

She was fiddling with the fastener of one of those beach-bags. We waited. She went on fiddling: then she stopped, and looked for some seconds blankly at a square, modernistic dolphin inset with viridian splendour into the red tiles of the terrace.

'Up guards and at 'em!' Harry said moving from one foot to the other. And as an afterthought: 'Eve!'

''Eave-oh!' I said shiftily.

Eve seemed to pull herself away from the dolphin, blinked up at us as if from sleep, smiled and started fiddling again. Then she suddenly stood up. 'Hold on,' she said, 'I won't be a moment.'

She went along the terrace into the hotel. Harry and I murmured the usual things about women. Then we just waited, looking idly about. In five minutes Eve came back. She walked more slowly, she passed

her hand over her brow in a tired way. She said to
Harry:

'Darling, I'm afraid I'd like to cut out of this.
D'you mind? I've got such a damned headache.'

Harry was really amazed. She had plainly said
nothing of this before.

'Headache?' he said. 'Headache?'

She looked at him with sudden meaning. A flash
between them, no more. 'Yes, darling. H-E-A-D . . .'

Harry became instantly fussy. 'Of course, of course.
You stay and rest. We'll go along together, won't we,
old boy?'

I felt very young and innocent. 'Of course we will.'

Harry was picking up bags and cameras and hats
in a flurry, muttering his 'of courses', and feeling
for something better he blurted out inconsequently:
'Can't spoil the ship for a ha'porth of tar, can we?'

Eve smiled: 'Darling, I *won't* be called a ha'porth
of tar.'

At which we all laughed. And soon she had waved
us a calm goodbye. But as we drove along our first
stretch of road, I found myself worried by some half-
recollection. For a long time I could not quite remember
what—then at last I had it. It had to do with a certain
air about Eve that morning. A brightness of the eye
beneath her assumed weariness, a sort of pouting of
the figure, a jauntiness even. An unusual radiance.
And I remembered when I had felt that particular
radiance from a woman, from women before. It came
when they gave me a kiss on their way to deceive me
with another man.

The tower was detestable. More exactly, dull. Just
a square erection, not very high, not very big, of local

stone. Old indeed, and with its top knocked off. Very plain. One could only stand in front of it and force oneself to think: 'All that time ago! All those dead people!' And blankly it stared back. But there was also a wide sandy café with a passable rosé; and an exquisitely placed restaurant with ordinarily rough tough food. There we sat for a long time and drank and looked out over the view of the hazed Surrey miles around. It was a hill-town, with planted trees and agaves and low cactus. Rising on its little mound, it was as though a true Provençal town had been set down somewhere near Oxley Heath on a bright blue summer's day.

We passed the day in wandering, in sleeping, and as the sun began to sink Harry found his game of boules—a scrappy one, hardly up to the magnificence of our Place, played by three youths on the hard bumpy clay of the old town's ramparts. This delayed us further, and we drove back a longer way to see more of very similar country. It was after six when we reached the hotel. Eve was out.

But she came in a few minutes later, effusive, happy to see us, still radiant. We know the old joke of the man who comes home with a blonde hair on the lapel of his coat. And there is the story of the girl in love with the miller's boy whose mother rebukes her for powdering too much: and of the lady in love with the fishmonger who covers her husband's pillow with the profits of her liaison, a silvery coinage of fishscale. Eve, who had not been near our car all day, was smeared—only a very little—with motor-grease.

That clinched the matter. But she seemed very happy to see us, she was not annoyed at having to

interrupt her afternoon, she was as affectionate and
pleased as if we had been two dearly-loved uncles
returned. Eve made a fuss of Harry that night, I
remember she took his arm once, and at dinner she
fussed over him with the food. A deeper suspicion
struck me—that she had been too thoroughly satisfied
with her afternoon to resent in any way her evening.

If one falls in love, or even imagines that one has
fallen in love, one is often beyond guilt. But not beyond
subterfuge. In the following days Eve continued to
make excursions to the village. To most people, had
they measured this with any mathematic, it would
have been impossible in such a small place to buy so
much: or to return so empty-handed. But Harry was
too interested in his boules and his other games to
notice anything. Besides, he was both trusting and
blind.

I did not see Eve with the garage-man again. I did not
exactly look for them, nor did I exactly close my eyes.
I took the middle self-deceiving way. I decided to
wander exactly where I wanted to wander on my own
account (how often my steps led me towards that bar
I cannot say)—yet at the same time I refused to keep
my eyes closed artificially for fear of seeing them. The
result of this was disquieting. I did not see Eve. But
I found that every third woman looked like her from
a distance. At the sight of every third woman's distant
back my heart gave a little extra thud. And I know
well that when one is in love, even a little in love, one
sees the image of the beloved in every distant shape:
hope contrives its mirage. And this complicated the
affair. Of course I remembered that in the beginning
I had openly found Eve attractive; I had even had

my short-lived hopes. But I did think that I had laughed these away. Now quite plainly I had been hiding from myself. I told myself not to be an old fool. But in one way I was glad. My snooping could no longer be classed with the curiosity of the lace-curtain: my underhand behaviour was prompted by an honest motive.

And Eve continued to come home smeared with oil. Here and there a small smear, a slight greyness like dust on her brown arm above the elbow, a small black spot on her leg, once an iridescence on the ankle that shone its mirage rainbow like an oiled puddle in the sun. Nothing outrageous, no more than these small flecks. It helped me that these evidences were part of comedy, it was easier for me to laugh down my own remote longing for her. Yet each time beyond their comedy I resented those evidences, and felt a far-off sadness, as if something had been stolen from me not then but a long time ago. I refused to let myself feel ambitious for Eve, as far as I was concerned she was irrevocably Harry's, and in any case experience told me that I would stand little chance with her. Nevertheless the longing remained, I had to face that, face it and try to forget it. I was in the position of a slightly sexy old uncle.

Somewhere in the nineteenth century, and mostly across the middle of Europe, there evolved a type of lady who can best be called a 'lionne'. She rode hard and she lived hard. Usually she was rich, or attached to wealth—otherwise she could not have followed her caprices with such fierce ease. At her best, she was a beauty and intelligent. I-don't-care was her talent, she was ruthless and romantic. Physically unafraid, she was afraid of hurting no-one. She was a golden beast.

She liked pistols, horses, balls to the dawn. She was restless, a storm of nerves, but she lived fast and hard in a glorious scornful way. Above all she never lacked courage.

Elizabeth of Austria is a clue to her. Today you may even see her poor residue in the motor-racing girl who likes her night-club. And now there came into Eve's life a kind of vital drive and a capricious energy that reminded me, enclosed in her own handsome shape, of the myth of the lionne. There was nothing very courageous she could attempt; but the same drive was there.

Whereas before she had been content to sunbathe and swim in the morning, now she quickly got to know a group of young Belgians who owned a hydro-plane. In this she went circling at speed far out on the calm blue; and soon she was behind them on a surf-board, head back, hair flying the spray, careless in the wind and speed. Once a motor-yacht, a streamlined modern water-mansion, anchored a long way off-shore. Eve was swimming round with us, and suddenly without a word started off towards it, she swam that long way out to it and after a while we saw her climbing up the rope ladder onto the deck. No marvellous feat— but part of the high-nerved energy, the wish for sudden decisions and a new ease with which she dealt with new people, that suddenly had changed her life. She stayed there quite a time and that evening a boat-load of mixed French and Americans came ashore, and Eve welcomed them and gave a sort of impromptu cocktail party. Which went on into the night and of which she was evidently the life and the soul. She behaved with elegance and fire, she was amusing and very gay. She took the wheel and drove us at terrible speed through the night to dance at a small Saturday bistro some miles away. We danced till it closed. Then she drove us to the nearest place along the coast where they had an all-night dive. Down in a cellar we sweated and played the fool till dawn. At dawn we bathed, and it was she who proposed it. Her carelessness was so sure, so certain and unafraid, that driving at such speed and on such suspect roads I did not feel at all afraid.

This kind of thing went on for several days. But she still went shopping in the afternoons.

One evening before dinner I was alone with her for a few moments, and she gave me a sudden sharp look. A look of serious censure. 'I hear you've been trying to change English money in the port,' she said.

'Me?' I said, hanging on for time.

'Yes you, my dear. Trying to outwit the poor natives?'

Her censure turned to a look of pure roguishness. She cocked an eyebrow and smiled knowingly like a nurse. 'And who is this girl friend you're hiding from us? This mysterious English?'

'I don't know what you're talking about.'

'This is a small place, you know.'

'All right, Eve—now who's been spinning you these atrocious indelicacies? Eh? Who?'

Eve put her finger to her lips.

'Ah,' she said.

So I just said 'Ah' back.

We prevaricated, and after more roguishness the matter was dropped. I was relieved. And discomforted. For here again was more evidence of her absolute lack of conscience. Never for a moment had she identified herself with the pound note and the bar. I found myself believing that even if the proprietor had suggested the lady was herself, she would still have found it absurd—why, *she* had never changed a note!—and would genuinely have argued with him. A moment's guilt, and her attitude would have been very different.

Everything led to the supposition that she was not flirting but riding deeply into love. I put aside the possibility that she was simply in love with the place, the south, the holiday. It must be more than that. And as I convinced myself, I grew further troubled. For apart from my own vague loyalties to Harry, apart from my stillborn personal jealousy of her, there was a further reason to hope the affair did not go too far. That was a simple enough one, but one most of us know—the simple fear of a scene, a violent and tedious eruption that would upset us and the tenor of our lives and lead to God would only know what.

So I thought that, as discreetly as I could, I had better stop speculating and find out the facts. It would be no more humiliating, no more dishonest to spy practically than to spy in mind.

And the next day after lunch I excused myself from the brandy and our new yachting friends, and strolled some way from the hotel. I hung about a side lane where there was a little bar and a communal washplace. Linen hung around me stiff in the hot sun. This was near the hotel garages too, and the whole place had an air of good daily work refreshing after the pleasure machine of our beach. I recommend the backs of hotels to all who on those coasts grow surfeited with life out front.

Presently Eve appeared on the way to her shopping.

At a careful distance I followed. Again the absurdity, the self-disgust of the snooper. In spite of my feeling for her, I cursed Eve for my humiliating rôle: in spite of my cursing, I had to admit that if anyone is to be followed let it be such a figure as Eve's. I once had a friend who was warned by an Italian policeman for wearing less than the official bathing dress on the sea-front at Rapallo: but that policeman took his time about it, he cycled for three hundred slow yards behind her before effecting his warning.

Not that Eve was much exposed—she wore a shirt and shorts—but her graceful long legs on their flat sandals, her exact straight back, her lack of all sway made an aloof and lovely precision. In the hot sun, walking like that, she looked cool.

Past the paper shop, a pause at the never changed row of English paperbacks, and quickly on. Past the dark leathern hole of the shoe-menders, past the sharp quincaillerie: and then no turn to the right where the body of the shops lay, but left to the garage. Yet at the garage no pause, she walked straight by and on towards the old church and the alleys of the port. Before reaching the port she stopped, still on the highway, and sat down on some sort of a stone thing. Within a few minutes the garage-man came along on a motor-cycle. There was no effusive greeting, and as if it were a habit Eve stepped across the pillion seat, steadied her hands on his waist, and they were off. I heard the machine's explosions long after they had rounded the corner, the open roar and the little bangs disappearing sadly into the faraway air.

It was over. They were gone. The street lay empty and disconsolate.

Empty myself, I simply walked slowly along, purposeless, aimlessly sober. I walked the way they, on their black little horse, had eloped: but slowly, wandering and no longer wondering.

The road, I remember, skirted the port and led along the coast, perhaps a half-kilometre inland. The sun ached, rough grey olive-trees twisted about the walls of the road, then the walls disappeared and only the thin strip of macadam twisted grey-black into the brush. There had been in that meeting something so settled, so intimately understood between two individual people, that I felt for the first time deeply and despicably that I had intruded upon a private matter. My road that afternoon was contempt.

I must have dawdled along a full kilometre when the road split in a fork. To one side the macadam continued on to the next village: to the left a gravelled track led towards the sea. This latter I took and soon, I remember, the arbutus and cystus that heathered about on either side ended, and I was walking into the curious moist aridity of a bamboo plantation. Suddenly Surrey had disappeared. No more the heathland, no more pines. No trees at all. But everywhere the thick-grown ranks of reedy bamboo, green leaves curling down like shade itself, like green cool paper. It looked dry, but you could smell the damp. It was a sudden tropic.

The hot afternoon silence weighed. At this hour no-one was abroad. It was the panic hour, and the bamboo grew just higher than my head, so that all around I had a hedge of green against the blue immense sky. No sound at all. Myself alone on the hot road, to left and right the un-nodding plumes of green motion-

less. I remember hearing my sandals on the gravel—
a small enough sound—and looking around carefully
all the time, as though the bamboo might at any time
close in if it were not watched. Even the insects slept.
No sound at all. The road surface ended—now there
were deep ruts and jagged rocks: no wheels could go
further, and I felt more and more as I walked on that
I was penetrating some forbidden wilderness from
which there could be no retreat.

As abruptly as it had begun it ended. It seemed afterwards a kind of purgatory through which one had to
pass to reach the heaven that lay beyond—a beach,
a treasure of a small secluded sandy beach. It was
empty, it was absolute. The water came in blue to the
sand, and to either side it hung emerald and mauve by
the protective rocks. The little lagoon was half-circled
by clustering miniature palm-trees—the palisade of
bamboo. And ahead only the blue magic of the horizon,
blue sky meeting blue water.

I stood there and breathed the clean air with great
blessed relief. Here was the real paradisial coast. Here
was pure southern magic, pure and drugged with sun.
Here was escape from the contemptible hour, from
those thoughts that seemed now to be left behind in a
squalid world beyond the bamboo grove, here at least
I could find peace from my intruder's mind.

I took off my clothes and walked into the clean blue
honey of the sea. Rich and cool it combed my body as
I swam, less like water than some buoyant cool jelly
it supported me as I lay upon its shape. But it smelled
of salt, and I filled my mouth with it and rinsed and
spat. So cool, so clear—and at last refreshed I came out
and laid myself down on the sand.

But it was too hot. I took my clothes up and looked around—no trees, but under the bamboo there was clear green shade. I walked over and stepped in among the reeds, and there, with the leaves bright green above me and bedded in a long grass that grew underneath, I made a pillow of my clothes and sank instantly to sleep.

When I awoke, Eve and her man were lying out there on the sand. They were naked and they were making love.

A cry, an insect, cramp—I don't know what woke me. My eyes near to the tall stems of grass, and the bamboo leaves above like trees—I thought I was away in some pleasant dream. And when through the grass I saw their two bodies alone on that sand, and recognized them, it seemed my mind had made an idyll of its food.

But not for long. In a real dream you can pretend to pinch yourself and agree: 'This is no dream, this is happening'. But in the live world you cannot really believe you are dreaming, all the senses all over the body that are asleep in a dream are undeniably awake. So I knew, really from the beginning, as soon as my whole body was awake, that what was there was real.

So clearly, not more than twenty feet away; and in such a shocked second I saw much more than I had seen of that beach before. Their bodies were near, large, they made the only movement there—but curiously this took no command of the picture, they were instead dwarfed by it. Two soft unshelled things against what could only now be seen as suddenly hardness all around. The mineral sand, the low rocks, the sea no more honey but hard blue salt: there was in the sea and the sky a great width—with only the bamboo palisade to measure height, and the sky right down on top of that, the beach was an insignificant speck on a great flat-land. Immensity stretched wide all round, it made an unprotected triviality of those two. And—why, because the eyes were abruptly so wide?— small things near them took sudden prominence, things I had never seen before in my first illusion of paradise, a dry yellowish wooden spar angled like a gibbet, a line of grey sand-plants straggling out from under the bamboo, a piece of pink cloth; the lances of bamboo flew their paper pennants brittle and knife-sharp, and in the quiet pools about those rocks the whole breeding marine life made itself felt, polyps, anemones, prawn-things and bright darting fishes. Everything turned sharp and dangerous against those two, soft-pink as shell-less crabflesh.

I was irrevocably there. I could make no movement. The bamboo stood so thick it was impossible to get further in without brushing up dangerous noise. I could only lie there. Even a movement of my head was dangerous—they might see what had been hidden before: and I could press it no nearer the earth. Then, as what was happening became clear, the first alert shock changed to sweating terror. I don't know now what kind of a terror it was, I don't know whether it was a shrinking after the first shock; or whether it was a true realization of my position; or horror for Eve or what else. But looking back I believe it was an animal terror, an intuition of natural mystery, perhaps not terror but frantic praise.

Then, as it must, the brain took over. It told me that I shouldn't be there, that no-one should intrude upon this sight that now suddenly became atrocious—and I closed my eyes tight. I shut them until I saw only black, buzzing black; but the effort was too great, the lids relaxed and my eyes lay there looking at the film of red where an outer golden light filtered through. Strange shapes occurred, dark hands passed across and violet amœbæ floated through sightless plasm. Behind, the dark mind ticked.

It ticked up anger. How dared they! How dared they risk this in that place where people might come! How could Eve prostrate herself in that atrocious way! What lunatic filth presumed in that man's upstart mind to lay a finger on her! What . . . and my eyes, with the fascination of disgust, were open again and looking at what seemed suddenly an odious sacrifice. Eve sacrificed with grey-blond hair strewn about the sand, that dark man an animal priest.

But then—for how many ways the mind can work at once, with what facility it races from image to image about the same scene, how it clothes and unclothes with variant idea its startled food—they began to look trivial, no longer soft against sharp dangers, no longer parts of some awed function, no longer distinguished by sacrifice—but simply two striving exercisers, awkward bodies performing an effortful acrobatic of the beach, froggish athletes about their work . . . I was forced to see the inexorable climax of romance—and since I was outside and I was not them it looked unbeautiful and absurd, and after no more than perhaps some seconds I closed my eyes, my eyes closed themselves willingly and under no more compulsion.

They would go, it would be over. Even if they saw me, even if that man saw me and in his surprise decided as he surely would that I had crept in from somewhere behind to watch them, even if in anger he protested—I felt I would never be moved, I'd feel it didn't matter, and if I felt at all then it would be scorn that I'd feel. No more alert, now weary, I lay for a long time with closed eyes, I even turned now slightly aside. Now and then suddenly I felt like murder. Then even this subsided and again I was left quiet, thoughtless, almost asleep. It was like lying quiet in a sick-room, after fever. The bamboo leaves made a pale ceiling, I counted and patterned them idly, I saw idly against this green ceiling the flickering of my own lashes as, almost closed, they feathered their own iridescence.

A long time later I shook myself from dozing and looked over there again. They had put on their clothes and lay there asleep. It was orderly. In sleep, sprawled with limbs at ease, curled even away from each other, they looked innocent. They, the beach, the sea itself had changed—an idyll of innocence now, two young people asleep on the sand by the sea. Eve's shirt was unbuttoned, one of her white breasts lay bare, the pale nipple a white smear in the sun. His sleeping hand that had covered it had fallen and lay palm upwards below it, fingers still outstretched—but in sleep gently, as a child might gently grasp but pause not knowing what it wanted.

Much later—for still I dared not really move, now for fear of waking them and of embarrassing Eve—I turned to look and they had gone: or they had nearly gone. I just saw their backs as they walked, arms linked, bodies swayed towards each other, through the opening in the bamboo. A few minutes later I heard from a long way off, like an echo of shooting from distant woods, the airblown rattle of that motor-cycle. I looked at my watch. It was six o'clock. Eve's habit was to return from the shops at half-past.

That evening I crept into the hotel by the back way —indeed, as I had left it. I could not face them. I left a note that I was following up something in the port, and that I'd not be in for dinner. Then I went out and found myself a small bar, and with slow satisfaction got drunk. As the brandy went down, and as I talked with half a mind about heaven knows what to a few workmen or fishermen there, things ceased to be bad. The matter was mollified. A sort of humour, or a hardness, mounted with the brandy; and with a drunk's dogma I remember repeating to myself, as though the phrase contained some profound and new truth, that Eve's one naked breast in the sun was the swellest thing on the riviera that year.

XII

IT was a morning of some confusion. Breakfast was out of the question, I slunk away alone to drink beer and cool my smoking flesh with a quiet bathe. It was a little better by lunchtime. But still shaky, such fierce flashing spots shot about my eyes that I had to wear dark glasses against their glare. And things happened in the corners of the eyes—a white cat flashed up and became a chair, strangely disconsolate music played that after an effort turned into the high moan of a vacuum cleaner.

People seemed to conspire to confuse. Behind me once, in a kind of small writing alcove in the hotel, a girl breathed frantically in the ear of a young man: 'But have you got a friend for *my* friend . . .?' I went through to the lounge, and there sat an elderly Frenchman who proclaimed slowly, as if to the air itself, in a weary but infinitely patient drone: 'With the Americans wanting to behave like the French and the French behaving like the Americans, what, my dear, are we to do?'

I retreated from this, but almost as if he had conjured her, an American lady whom we knew as a fellow guest cornered me brightly and, after some morning preliminaries, asked, perhaps to please me after my dull answers: 'I've often wanted to have you tell me—do you write in point of fact on a machine or d'you utilize a pen?' I told her—and fled. I left by a side door and sat sternly by myself on a garden seat. But soon, from behind a clump of oleander, a small

British voice said: 'Bye Bye'. And this was echoed by a still smaller voice: 'Bye Bye'. A chuckle, and then, with elfin delight, as though this was the epigram of all time, as though no changes evermore need ring, the first voice took a breath and said louder: 'Bye Bye!' And the still smaller voice, over-brimmed with pleasure, answered 'Bye Bye'. This went on for some minutes: 'Bye Bye'. 'Bye Bye'.

Pan-voices of the noon-day hush! I leaned a little aside and peered through the thin oleander leaves. A small girl was entertaining a smaller girl in a pram. They were only a foot away from each other, waved their hands in each other's faces, and repeated always to each other: 'Bye Bye! Bye Bye!' I withdrew on tiptoe—less from fear of disturbing them than of being myself drawn into that giddy, endless, circular ritual.

So that by lunchtime, when I met Eve and Harry, I was still not sure that things were exactly what they seemed to be. And there was Eve, cool and charming and untouchable, in a fresh cool dress with her hair coolly brushed, exactly in fact as she always had been, unchanged whatsoever. It seemed impossible. It seemed in my muzzed head I must have dreamed that scene. This aloof and fragrant friendly woman had nothing to do with the other, that other one sprawled in the hot sand. As may happen after alcohol, the mind grew suspicious of magic motives around, of intricate processes at work—and I found myself wondering whether Eve, herself such a creature of her own illusion, was not at work creating illusions? But I told myself not to be a fool, that the act of love was an experience of beauty, and not at all as it might look—in fact that I was dramatizing everything out of

its proportion. Yet theorizing is different to believing
—and as we lunched, and I stole glances at Eve, I
could not wholly believe that curious heaven among
the bamboo had ever existed.

I kept away from the port that afternoon, and because
of this met Harry later in the Place. There was an important concourse of boules. Players from neighbouring
towns had arrived. All over the wide sandy stretch of
the Place these were grouped at the end of their pitches,
and spectators thronged each game in long excited
ranks. Great excitement, and a great variety of faces—
all the slow-living, hardworking life of southern com-
merce seemed to have closed down for the afternoon.
Notaries jostled farmers, agents for vineyards retorted
with itinerant Algerians, Italian faces spoke with
French, armless veterans of old wars argued the game
with beach-clad youngsters . . . it was all a violent
vibrant mix-up, all sun-baked wine-caked hot cloth
and brown skin. But still conspicuous, and taller than
others, stood the formidable English figure of Harry in
his long khaki shorts, his white stockings, his ranger's
shirt with its empire-building pockets. He stood erect
and stiff; and still about him clung that invisible
overcoat.

We watched together for some time—Harry applaud-
ing the dexterities and twists, and painedly decrying
so much excitement and argument. But that afternoon
he was not playing himself, and after a while he suddenly turned to me and said: 'Hell, let's go for a walk.'

Then added: 'Let's go to that port you're so fond of,
I've never had a proper decko round there. Any fishing
go on?'

I don't know whether this was the first time he had

suggested it: but it felt like it. I was panicked. Then I tried casually: 'The port? Not much doing there really . . .'

'But you always go there yourself? I'd like to see what you see in it. Unveil the secret and all that.'

He was choosing his words well. I tried his mercy: 'The truth is, Harry, I've been there so much I've got a bit fed up. I mean for instance, that's why I'm here today. Got browned off with the place.'

'Oh.'

He paused. Then: 'Anyway, we're going back to the hotel—let's just walk back that way. Don't suppose I'll see what you see in it, you can shut your eyes if you like—blind leading the blind, eh?'

We stood there in the heat with the little balls cracking all around us. It brought my hangover nerving back, and that suggested a lie: 'Well, *really* the truth is I got myself nicely drunk there with a crowd of—of locals—and I don't think I dare show my face today. Nothing wrong, mind you . . . just jitters.'

He looked at me, twinkling a bit, shrewd a bit: 'Certainly seem to have a lot of different truths in you today, old man. Bit dubious, aren't you?'

'Well . . .'

'Why didn't you say so in the first place?'

We were walking away. He seemed to have forgotten. But once he muttered thoughtfully: 'Mysteries'. It sounded ominously as if he really knew something and was dwelling on it; but at least we walked on and straight to the hotel.

He started talking about the boules, I listened with half an ear but I was thinking with new dismay: 'Now I'm definitely in collusion with Eve. I've helped to hide

the thing up—should I have done that? Why have I
done that? Why not just let it ride and let Harry find
out by chance if chance should wish it, let matters take
their natural course? What should I do? Who in hell
am I loyal to?'

I began thinking of the past with Harry, past holidays,
holidays of our youth. He himself had always been
what can only be called 'one for the girls': something
above a 'ladies' man' and below a 'wolf'. I can remember Harry and myself playing cricket on the sands with
a little girl who stands out clearly, and always with a
mysterious wonder, in my memory: we were all about
four or five, and we were both in love with her. That
was an early enough start—and again some years later,
sometimes when we were feeling our first long trousers,
there were two boyish bobbed-haired gamesters we
used to paddle about in some boat in some green
estuary: those were the days of picnics and touchless
love, for we had not thought then of kissing—though
letters that came in term-time were judged, with wonder
and hopeless mystery, by the amount of crosses they
carried beneath the girl's sweet signing name. Always,
as we grew up together, there were girls—and the
romances of sea and holiday. And there came a time
when we ceased to go away with our parents, we chose
our own summers—formidably we left sea-villages of
our boyhood days for the little towns where 'something
might be going on': that something, of course, was
girls. Sometimes we struck lucky, but often on those
desolate grey promenades we wandered alone, with
empty pockets and full hearts, while the sad orange
sun struck the seaside façades with its grim tale of
another day gone, another day lost. Bitterly, whenever

I see the dying fire of the summer sun on white tiles, I seem to remember, though I cannot quite place it, some sort of a white-tiled café where once we must have passed our lonely evenings: it was in a narrow street, a hill-street that led down to the sea—with mysterious promise the sea lay open at its end; there were long green lilies on those tiles, and in the westering sun they are the saddest thing I can remember. Those tiles—and the smell of wet sand at the death of a seaside day. But it was not always like that—there was one unbelievable night when, walking home alone along the promenade after some luckless night in a dance-hall, a sports-car drew up beside us and in it were two quite pretty girls who asked us to go for a drive on the downs and help them drink the beer they had. We did: and it is unlikely that either of us has ever felt quite so hopeless since.

In all, Harry's life seemed to me to have been patterned with romance and sex. It was very possible that since his marriage he had decided, and rightly wished, to be true to Eve: but how did I *know* that? I still found it difficult really to believe that given a safe opportunity this man whom I had known so much as a 'bit of a dog' would not secure for himself, almost guiltlessly, almost morally, his 'bit of fun'. I could not quite convince myself that I owed him loyalty in this affair of Eve's. Again the two problems presented themselves—wash my hands of it, even send myself a false telegram to go home: or intrude with some positive move to stop the whole business. But then what?

At dinner this was decided for me.

We were talking amiably of nothing much—it must

have been about the Belgians who had just left and about the end of Eve's aquaplaning and so forth—when Harry suddenly said to Eve: 'At any rate, I hear you've taken to a motor-bike.'

A second of silence. Within it, small dreadful sounds —Eve's sudden gasp, my hand somehow gripping knives and clattering them against my plate. For the first time for days I saw her crumpled—she just stared at him pale. Harry frowned: 'Heavens alive—what's the matter? Seen a ghost?'

Then Eve caught herself and said too steadily, with something of the steady tone of a real drunk: 'Motor-bike? How motor-bike?'

Harry was puzzled, and when he was puzzled his eyes grew shrewd and very watchful: 'I take it you're shocked that the peasants have observed you astride such a machine? But an acquaintance of mine in the town, an individual in the way of business, a shoe-maker, and a fine boules-thrower to boot, informed me . . .'

'For God's sake, darling, go on. . . .'

Harry pressed his lips together and went on as slowly, firmly, severely as he wanted: '. . . informed me—no, asked me how Madame enjoyed her perambulations with her "ami" on his motor-bicyclette. Very sportive, he said, les anglaises. But I don't know that I approve of my wife deporting herself in such a manner.'

Again silence, and he looked up curtly at Eve. She had that schoolgirl look again—found out, caught.

She was deeply terrified—she must have missed a well-known twinkle somewhere in Harry's face. But I saw it, and I suppose making some absurd sound, I succeeded in bursting with laughter. I remember making the theatre gestures—holding my sides, pretending I had choked myself.

Eve looked at me with disgust. Harry, trying to keep the severe face he found so funny, started to smile.

I thought hard then of Harry's bad French, how with luck what must have been some shopkeeper's malice could not have been thoroughly understood. I spluttered: 'God, what a sight for them—I've only just seen it—Eve on the Vicar's Daughter!'

'The Vicar's Daughter? So it was you?' Harry laughed.

I spoke then suddenly clearly, separating the words as if I were sending her a telegram: 'Yes-I-took-her-for-a-spin-on-the-Vicar's-Daughter.'

Eve just sighed: 'Yes, the Vicar's Daughter.' She knew very well, and she knew I knew, that she had never been on the thing.

She looked over at me with what I had hoped might be love, or loving thanks—but was instead a kind of compassion. She looked sorry for me. It must have been her sorrow for herself printed on a face too relieved to express more.

But the air was still charged. And now Harry felt this too. He said: 'You never told me.'

'About a ride on that thing?' I said. 'Hardly makes a story.'

He looked from one to the other of us and quietly repeated: 'But you never *told* me.'

I had never before seen him look shifty. Something had put him off balance. I felt suddenly it might be the faint breath of suspicion that Eve and I had something in common together—a romance of our own.

He looked at us again and muttered: 'Mysteries . . . mysteries . . .'

That was too much. He might know we had something together—but his solution was so preposterous it cleared the air, and I was able to speak easily at last:

'Mysteries my foot! What on earth are you talking about? You spend half your time playing tennis and half your time watching those ridiculous little balls dribbling up and down the sand. But you don't come back from your tennis and tell us word for word what games and sets you won or lost—at least you *do*, more's the pity. But hell, one can't repeat all the little things that happen during the day here . . . it's all so various one'd be talking all night! And boring you to death! Mysteries, indeed!'

He looked very surprised, I suppose I had spoken vehemently—but he seemed to relax. He must have been thinking, with a certain complacence, how worked up these writer-fellows get. Then he said good-naturedly: 'I suppose you're right, old man. I do rather bury myself.'

Eve said nothing, but I could almost hear her thinking. Just then a waiter brought more wine, and while this was being poured Harry went on: 'Silly to pay out all this dough and not get to know the place more. I'll make a point of looking round.'

I took a deep breath. 'Harry,' I said, 'I think we all need a blow. Why don't we go along the coast for a night—Cassis, even Marseilles? Yes, Marseilles.'

Harry looked over to Eve. 'What d'you say?'

I think she saw it was best to clear out for a moment,

Harry might speak to his gossiping shoe-maker again. But she had to say: 'Not go for good?'

'No no,' I said. 'Just for a night.'

'Make a change,' Harry said.

Eve tried to be gay: 'Then I'm all for it. Soon as poss. Tonight?'

Harry laughed. It was all easy now. 'And drive all night? I like my bed. Let's go tomorrow.'

Then he frowned: 'And talking by the way, of going . . . when *are* we going to go? It's been three weeks now. . . .'

And then began a council of war. Money, time, responsibilities at home were all discussed. We had not before talked so seriously of this. The last weeks had been lived in Mediterranean air, with all its glamours and all its indifferences—and drenched in this it was surprising to realize again that I was sitting not with two aimless sophisticates but in the arms of a respectable middle class. Whatever the riviera made them look like, whatever it had made them do, these people were nevertheless the beginnings of a small rock in the sandy Surrey heathland, these were a family, steady livers, builders of nice-style homes and lupined gardens. They were 'nice' people.

We found that money presented no serious difficulty, no more than at home: only time might threaten us. Harry certainly could not extend his leave too long— though at his office this had been recognized as a sort of honeymoon and holiday combined. And the idea of the house at Oxley called him. Finally we found we had a week and at the most ten days more.

Eve tried to argue. She was plainly disappointed and made no attempt to hide it. She loved the place, it would be awful to go back to England and prepare to face what one imagined of England's beautiful autumns—rain and grey skies. It seemed she had forgotten the danger she now courted—or she had got her second wind and trusted that somehow she could avoid it. So she made quite a fuss, she appealed to Harry—but he was firm. I must add, though, that at no time did she suggest that he should go back alone. Soon she excused herself and went early to bed.

I remember Harry looking after her amusedly, like a parent. 'She's such a little girl,' he said.

The next day, early, we left for Marseilles. But first Harry insisted on filling up with petrol. So we drove into the garage.

It was the first time I had taken a considerative look at Eve's young man. When he saw the car he hurried away into the dimness of the sheds, and it was the proprietor himself who came to serve us at the pump. I did not look at Eve, I don't know whether she went white or what she did—but I determined to swallow my own feelings and to have a look at that young man. I got out on some pretext and found him bent over a tool-bench at the back of the garage.

I asked him for a match. As he handed me his lighter he said nothing, but his eyes watched me carefully, he was on his guard. But I spoke with forced affability— and the moment he saw that I was not suspicious he became charming indeed.

He was a well-set-up young fellow with straight black hair. He was not very brown. His cheekbones were high and wide, and his black eyes tried to be almond-shaped, they were a little caught up at the ends of the lids. He had that sort of French face that seems almost to be a face drawn upon a face—lips so moulded, eyebrows so exact. Lips moulded, but thin— with an easy smile that showed many small white teeth and was not unsatanic. But he had a pleasing, and a pleasure-willing, personality: he was manly and strong. Altogether, I could not help liking him.

When I said casually that we would all be going north in a week, he did not look at all troubled. 'Yes?' he smiled politely: and nodded in the way people nod when told of a journey, as though no more pleasant prospect could ever be. It did not seem to be a good omen for Eve, and I hoped that she had only lost her body to him and not her heart.

Then I told him we were off to Marseilles imme-diately. And to give him his due his face did fall—for a moment, for a millimetre.

XIII

THESE days so many of one's friends spend their holiday on the southern coasts of France that a chance meeting can no longer be called coincidental; or, for that matter, chance. The only magic left in this situation is that if you are alone and hoping to meet someone, coincidentally you don't. So that late that afternoon, since we were not looking for Roddy Meredith on the Canebière, we found him.

He was in a large basket-chaired café, a café as cool as a club. His table was stacked with newspapers and brochures; he gave the impression of a violent man of affairs. I did not at first realize it was Roddy when Eve gave her opening squeak of recognition. She made noises of astonished delight, she primped us over to Roddy with all the posturing, like a dove stamping out its love-dance, of one person meeting another. Harry stood behind, a politely gruff guardian. Roddy, as usual, would have none of it: disdaining even to say hello he looked fiercely at Eve and said:

'Tunis is a woman.'

'But Roddy, how *extraordinary*,' Eve cried, 'to find you here!'

'And Algeria as we all know is a man. And Morocco is a warrior.'

'We had no *idea* you'd be here!'

'So why do I want to go to Tunis?'

'Think of it—just walking along the street and—'

Roddy smiled wicked benevolence and said in the

tones of a comfortably ending fairy tale: 'I'll tell you why—it's because I've never *been* there.'

Eve said how small the world was and Roddy told her please to sit down and rest: and so we all sat and drank cool drinks against the hot gritty crowd of the Canebière. The great port lorries thundered past, whistles of dark-skinned gendarmes screamed like birds in a metal jungle, a deep boom of some steamer from Africa sounded from the grim blue water of the Château d'If. We sat for a long time and chattered about ourselves, and the soft-shoed predatory crowd streamed the pavement two ways past. Roddy, it turned out, was taking the next day's plane to Tunis.

It was some time after five, and we went for a walk down by the Vieux Port. Across the wide tramlines, round black hulls of oiled boats and into a small fair where officers of the French-African army sat like children in a device of small electric cars. Then back again to the opposite waterfront of sea-food sellers. I think it was about there that Roddy and Harry had strolled on in front and Eve and I were for the first time alone together since that talk of the motor-cycle.

As soon as we were alone she stopped talking. She was plainly trying to dare to speak of it. But there was a moment only—one knows well those walks when a moment later others may join back again—and she suddenly whispered:

'How did you know?'

'I saw you—obviously.'

'Where?'

The others had stopped to look at something—we stopped too, and stood there faced with an unusual blue tubby boat whose tall thin funnel was rigged as a mast, but through which smoke still poured. There was little time, it was urgent, Eve had urgently to know how much I knew. The word 'bamboo' was on my lips, but of course I could not speak of that.

'Well,' I said. 'You hardly hid yourself. I saw you once or twice going off with him on that motor-bike. It wasn't hard to see you were rather more than friends.'

She said nothing, not looking at me, waiting, listening so hard:

'And of course I saw you in that little bar by the church—*you* were my fictitious girl friend of that bar, Eve.'

She stubbed about with her toe: 'Lord, what a fool I've been,' she whispered.

It sounded, the way she whispered it, penitential. I felt an enormous relief.

'So it's not serious?' I said.

She looked up carelessly—with a look of something taken so for granted it is not worth discussion.

'Oh it's serious,' she said. 'I meant what a fool I was not to be more careful about it. I'd forgotten you went to the port. I only thought of Harry.'

Then she turned and touched my arm: 'Oh, but it was so kind of you.'

That was awkward. It only seemed to seal matters, to pronounce them valid.

'But Eve,' I said—and how that flagstaff funnel belched smoke against the blue sky!—'But Eve, what's the good? You'll have to leave him.'

'But I won't,' she started to say, 'you see . . .'

And then there was Harry hurrying back with what

looked like an old hairy piece of mud in his hand. He was holding it out and laughing: 'Know what this is called?' he said. 'Come and look!'

He grabbed Eve's arm and still chuckling hurried us along to a sea-food stall. There among baskets of urchins and oysters lay a basket of pieces of hairy mud. Some had been opened—and inside the mud was a long shell and inside this a disgusting gobbet of rubbery yellow stuff. Above, a label proclaimed with pride: 'Violets de Marseilles.' Eve began to shake with laughter, quietly; then she laughed out loud and went on laughing, shaking her shoulders as if she were sobbing. She went on long after we others had stopped. And as we walked off to a restaurant she kept starting to laugh again.

Marseilles, with pavements and cobbles not sun-pale like other southern towns but dark grey; Marseilles whose function is that of a lively heavyweight, whose people are grimed and gritty and make no elegant pretensions; Marseilles of great docks and great railways and her funiculared cathedral—Marseilles can be very hot: and at her hottest after too many oysters and a large indigestible dinner. It may have been these two heats inside and outside that first conjured up for me the lovely word 'oasis'. I saw it written in my mind—green, fertile, shady, cool. It looked wonderful. Then next to it appeared Roddy's plane, whirling its own cool wind to Tunis—itself a word of soft perfumes, and where oases themselves grow green. Suddenly I saw it all might fit, and I turned and said quietly to Harry:

'Why don't we all take that plane?'

'What plane?'

'To Tunis. Tomorrow.'

We were sitting in a dancing bar over our tired brandies. Roddy and Eve were dancing. Harry was moodily watching the tarts—indeed a moody sight, for some were very young and beautiful, and while they danced and flirted with the wealthy men whose wine they drank, occasionally their pimps looked in at the door and made signs, one of them a soiled Algerian with a dead eye-socket and a look of disease. Coloured lanterns hung garish about the red-wood walls, a band played American jazz, and life was lively at a lively cost.

Harry looked at me amazed. Then squinted down at my glass—and smiled.

'No,' I said, 'it's not the drink.'

'T-ew-nis?' Screwing up his eyes.

'We've got the time and the money—we've talked about that. And you wanted a blow. Why not a heavier blow?'

'But what about our things? Clothes and whatnot?'

'You don't need any. You can get what you're wearing washed. We've got our cases for the night.'

'I might get a letter of recall. It's very possible.'

'You're hedging.'

'Well—I might—'

'Might?'

'Well what about the car?'

'Marseilles has spectacular garages.'

'But supposing—what about the planes back?'

'We can check that.'

'But have you ever *been* there?'

'No. Have you?'

'No. I mean, anything might happen . . .'

'Three or four days and we'd be back. We'd have

seen something really different. *And* you could have the car overhauled. You know, Harry, I think the car needs a good look over before we drive north.'

'Yes—something in that—'

'It'd be hell if we broke down.'

'Mm.'

'After some of these secondary roads. You never know.'

'Lot in what you say.'

He was beginning to think now. And then the band stopped playing. I put a finger to my lips: 'Not a word to the others—shh for the moment!'

He looked surprised, began to say something, then stopped bewildered and thoughtful as Roddy and Eve came sweating and laughing back to the table.

'I'm setting Eve up in business here,' Roddy said. 'There's a gaz-and-pneu baron from Bormes has only eyes for her. . . .'

'Roddy, do shut up. . . .'

'A paunch worth fifty thousand, something a girl can get her teeth into . . .'

'I'll set *you* up in business.'

'My dear!'

And for some minutes that sort of thing, never repeatable but funny at the high time. Harry sat there saddled with his thoughts. Suddenly he smiled to himself, and I breathed easier. Then the band started a little whistling, arpeggios on a piccolo, and everybody looked to see what this could be—when drums and maraccas abruptly crashed into a South American rhythm and Roddy was up, delighted to be able to waggle to this, Eve was away with him, and Harry could say:

'It would be a bit of a show, wouldn't it?'

'It would.'

'Then I'm on, old man.'

'And Eve?'

He wrinkled: 'I think I know why you shushed me just now. A surprise, eh?'

'A surprise.'

'That's the ticket . . . not a word . . . now let's get down to the business side.'

The upshot was that the next morning I stole out early to the air office and bought by the grace of a cancellation and other more persuasive measures three tickets on Roddy's plane. Later we offered Roddy a lift to the airport (to save him waiting about for the official busload) and I lured Eve in to the airport bar while Harry unloaded the bags and drove the car to the garage. He got back in good time.

Then there in the airport hall, on smooth concrete and by little clumps of bags, among sad groups of travellers and to a thunder of engines from the airfield outside—there came the dreadful, the bright deadly moment, the high-spirited oh-what-madmen-are-we moment when we broke Eve's future.

She was hopelessly crushed. She made no fight. She was beaten. The others took it for surprise.

XIV

HIGH over the blue sea, past the marshy maps of Corsica and Sardinia, then the coast of brown Africa. Harry sat with Eve, he had his arm round her, he must have thought her white face meant airfright. Sometimes I saw her face turn to his and smile an ashamed smile, a smile after tears—though I don't think she ever cried. I sat with a plump brown lady in black who smelled alternatively of quite clean sweat and a strong and most exquisite perfume—'C'est moi' the one, 'A toi' the other. Roddy sat away in front, a baby strung over him in a hammock.

We touched down at Tunis airport, and as we climbed down the little ladder onto Africa some dozens of flies touched down on us. These, or others like them, small pale stingless ticklers, were to remain with us throughout the days ahead. We were charged with their company into Tunis, thence into the train that was to take us some kilometres down the coast Sousse-wards to the sea-village where Roddy had arranged to stay. It was a train of square wooden carriages, and we sat in a dining-car of varnished planks and brilliant brass—with its fezzed waiters it might have been the stateroom of the Bey's steam-yacht itself. It was very hot. We kept stopping at dusk-ridden stations where mysterious white shapes moved. Eve kept calling for more brandy—usually she drank little—and in spite of whatever went on in her mind she brightened up. When at last we arrived at the white plain beautiful hotel it was night, the flies had gone, and we were all—in Harry's words—in cracking good form.

We dined in a garden of grey pebbles and great trumpet-shaped red flowers, among feathery trees and palms, with jasmin bunches in our hands to sniff and a great lazy fragrance all around—we dined off a great herbed fish and rice-bound lumps of chicken and a mound of sweet white nut-cake and much else at half the cost of France. Arab music whined from a radio back among the white geometry of house-shapes, a donkey brayed its rubber lament like an old motor-horn, camels frayed like weathered rope splayed past on their precise matronly feet, a cat stalked a great green mantis—at last we had settled somewhere Surreyless.

But I knew it was much of a lull before a storm. A storm of which I was to receive the main force.

We must have got through that great meal quite quickly, for the road that separated the hotel from the sand and the sea was still a movement of beasts and people by the time we rose to go to our rooms and unpack. There was nothing much to unpack, and I remember looking rather blankly round my white-washed room and wondering what to do: I went out onto the balcony, and the sounds of the road drew me down. I thought I would take a stroll.

I walked a few yards down the road, away from the light thrown by the hotel windows; and just outside that light was another world—a white and black moonlit world, white houses and white sand and black shadows and black sea: women passed me muffled in white, dark-clothed men became black. Only over by an immense old fort was there yellow light—a lighthouse beacon, winking like a clock, and the reflected light of an Arab café on its great sandy walls. Then Eve was by my side—white: and strangely, with the murmur of red that roses maintain in the night, her rouged lips shone red the only colour round. She was beautiful, beautiful.

'You bloody swine,' she said.

'You filthy bloody spy, *you* fixed this!' her lips said.

'You —, what the bloody hell do you mean by poking your —ing nose in where it's not bloody wanted . . .?

'You —! You —! You . . .'

On and on she swore those words, on and on the words came spitting from inside her where they had lain hidden since some back-stage life of long ago. An Arab passed slowly urging 'Arra! Arra!' to his mule.

Her teeth were clenched white in the red round of her lips. She broke off for breath in a sob.

I think I must have just said: 'Eve!' Or perhaps nothing.

She got her shaking breath and went on: quicker, too quick to curse: 'You've been spying snooping prying ever since I set eyes on you *I* know why you asked me to your flat *I* remember you following me in Chelsea that night *I* know your bloody ways *I* know you've been creeping about that port watching and following and prying and now you've gone and fixed me into this god-damned hole, you've *spoiled* it—you think you have but you're wrong, you're wrong you cow-eyed fool oh yes I've seen your bloody eyes on me too . . .'

She broke down sobbing and suddenly clung to my

arm, clung for help, and she moaned only: 'Oh why did you do it, why did you *do* it?'

Can one lay a hand on those who cry? Can one give sympathy? Can one pat a shoulder? I remember feeling so terribly sorry, I think I only wanted to cry too—but I was outside it, I wanted most for it to be over, I waited awkward and knew all the time what was going on round us. Two small bedouin boys had come up with bouquets of jasmin, and thinking us lovers, stood postured like little whores rolling hashish eyes and holding up their bunches of white flower-buds.

Jotas in the throat. *Jasmin . . . Jasmin . . .* And I who had been about to defend myself, and had rejected that as needless, found myself just muttering 'There, there.' And she went on sobbing and I said: 'You do really love him then?'

I felt a nodding in my arms.

'And you're sure it's not just romance, a deep romance?'

She shook her head, the hair shook to and fro.

'Jasmin? Voulez Jasmin?'

I tried to beat them away with my free hand. They just laughed.

'But Eve, what's going to happen? What about the future?'

She shook. Something sobbed up like: 'Hang the future!'

'You can't just . . .'

'I—I can . . .'

Jasmin . . . Jasmin . . .

I tried gently to move her away from me. Two Arabs were squatted in the sand a few yards away, watching impassive as wise old children. They never

moved their eyes off, indolently they munched us. I
said more firmly, but I think sadly too:

'You can't help it, Eve. You're going back to
England, he's staying here. The future'll—'

She took herself away; stopped sobbing; said breath-
lessly: 'But he's not stopping here!'

'What?'

'He's—you see, he's only here for the summer,
waiting. He's a pilot. He's got a job in the autumn.
He's flying—f-freight from France to England. Sometimes he'll come near to London. Freight.' She seemed
to titter. 'Doesn't that sound silly—*freight*?'

So that was that.

Jasmin . . . *Jasmin* . . . echoed like a sarcastic laugh
behind us.

We turned and walked back to the hotel.

Before she left me Eve smiled and touched my arm
again tenderly, with hope: 'You were kind to say
nothing to Harry. Thank you.'

'I was only thinking of myself.'

Which I saw then quite clearly for the first time to
be absolutely true. But it sounded so boorish a return
to her thanks that we both made a face against the
words.

Then like a white shadow she vanished in the dark.

The next days were bad and brittle. Knowing too
much, ashamed of it, rotten with innuendo I started
drinking and talking and laughing too much. Eve,
who had the job of containing herself, did the same.
Roddy's intuition quickly told him that something was
up, and I suppose liking to be excited got high with

G*   193

us too. Harry joined in—the village offered no sport
for him, he was I think stirred by the idea 'Africa',
his eyes twinkled and his chuckles told us he was
genuinely pleased by the family conspiracy of fun
with wife and two friends in this strange place. Once
or twice—for one must remember that Harry though
a little blind was no fool—I caught him puzzled. He
had sensed that something was up, but since he knew
none of the facts he must have resigned the matter
to drink and the slow African air.

Beneath our brittle playing moved a mild cafard.
It was hot and sultry, long yellow clouds drifted about
a sky now blue, now grey. The mind grew soft, one
forgot things—one moved from one room to another
and forgot why. It was difficult to write even a post-
card. And all day the flies were tickling us, we went
about armed with absurd flit-guns: 'Will you flit *me*
if I flit *you*?' The flies settled down on us and walked
about and rubbed their legs all day. And there was
another, and most important confusion—the Arab life.
There one is—suddenly set down among a people of
whom one can know absolutely nothing—what they
are doing, saying, thinking, hoping, mourning. It is
usually possible to approximate what might be going
on in a European's mind—however remote he is. But
here where religion and moral and ethic are all different, everything is confusion, the feeling of ignorance
is absolute—however many books one might have read.

Dazed, we drank anisette and became more dazed.
We drank in the bar with a few French functionaries
or up on the broad private balcony leading from our
rooms. There, stretched on chaises-longues of white
wicker, with the sea and the sand stretched in front

and the road making strange noises beneath, we poured out the white stuff and sweating and silly idled away the days. I find I have written down in an old note-book what seemed so funny then. Over a map of Tunisia, we agreed that it's no Sousse if you don't get your Sfax right. Dried up river beds were held to be the result of Ouedsday Early Closing.

Songs were contrived and sung. We cheated about flying from Marseilles instead of Nice and to a New-Yorkish tune sang:

> 'I gotta Date in Tunis
> And so adieu to *you* Nice,'

—and then something else and back to the theme:

> 'I gotta Date in Tunis—
> That's where the clair-de-lune is,
> I'm on the trail
> Of an ouled nupti-äil,
> And so it's souks, souks, souks to you Nice
> For I gotta Date in Tunis.'

I seem to remember—and memory brings the smell of anisette and jasmin and the nut-oiled Arab cooking—that there was some other pun on rubbing one's bum with Bay Rhum and lubbing, honouring and oh-oh-Bey-ing. And this last led to a witful rumba outside the Tunisian orbit, on the heroic lines of Havana Hannah and Trissie from Trinidad:

> 'From the Isle of Man
> To the Isle Love You
> There's not a better lay-oh
> Than a one-man Sodom
> (Podden me modom)—
> Charlie the Cicisbeo.'

At which the band would drop their instruments (the flit-guns) to chant a reprise:

> ' Love, Honour and Obey-oh
> Charlie the Cicisbeo.'

And since such moods compound, and grow always wilder, the Tunisian night soon resounded as if a Canterbury of Cossacks had moved in to the high choral:

> 'Sing Hoch for the Heil of Wight!
> Sing Malte Laurids Brigge!
> You can't have It and eat your cake,
> Your figure just gets bigger.'

To such heady music Eve hennaed her hair, she sloshed henna's green mud all over the bedroom floor and stood in it with the green cement on her head like a bronze Greek casque. Once I tried to read a book on the tyrant Ibrahim Ibn Ahmed, whose atrocious cruelty was attributed to a 'portentous secretion of black bile'—but soon gave that up. And meanwhile through moonlit nights lunatic cocks crowed from the white mirage of domes—and the mules themselves became a mirage, one was bright pink and all were ridden by Arabs wearing wide-brimmed straw hats that made them Mexicans and the mules burros. For a long time it was uncertain what the Arab ladies looked like—they wore white cowled robes leaving only a small circle for their face, which was mostly covered with a short black veil: not quite a nun in negative, not exactly an oval Venetian mask—and in a moment of inspired relief it became finally clear that they looked like nothing more than Liquorice-All-Sorts. And red fezzes and tasselled fezzes walked about, and great moustached mussulmen with jasmin-draped ears, and tattooed Bedouins in their blue robes, and a Moroccan doctor in trousers cut like yacht-sails, and bundles of white wool that were peasant women, and large bundles of faggots that seemed to have nobody carrying them, and great fishing-nets stalking the beach, and a Turkish swimmer gleaming with muscle—and always the braying of mules and the grunt of camels and the Arra! Arra! of drivers and the whining of an Arab radio and forever the flies.

So it was against such confusion that we grouped our frivolous white indolence on that perfumed verandah. But it was only perhaps the second day of this that a further development occurred. In the exhausted silence after some peak of fooling, a distant look came into Eve's eyes, a little smile played on her lips: 'Thank God there aren't any scorpions here,' she said. 'I was nearly stung by a scorpion once.'

Harry cocked up an eye: 'You?'

'They're horrid things, the way their tails go up— ugh . . .'

'But you've never been near a scorpion, Eve!'

'That's all you know. That uncle of mine used to bring them back from his trips. Scorpions. Snakes too.'

'For God's sake, *what* uncle?'

'Uncle Hugo. He was oh, an explorer, or in the Legion or something. Didn't I ever tell you about him? He was an extrordinary man—'

Harry pursed his lips and looked down while Eve described the feats of Uncle Hugo. We all knew she was at it again. It seemed a voice from very long ago. We had not had a story from her since she had left England. I suppose since the new charm of reality had reached a full fruition at our town in France, it was as fully destroyed here however colourful Tunis chose to make herself. Eve was lonely now, and she wanted something —and the old technique for supplying this rolled smoothly into action.

We all waited patiently while she finished. I will not repeat the story, it was like any of the others, it claimed a conventionally romantic upbringing and an elderly affectionate male-figure as all the others had done. Harry sighed once, although he had resigned himself to her fantasy, he must have seen that he had only been given a holiday these past weeks, and that the effort must be made, like a return to life after a holiday, all over again. And the next day, or sometime after, we were given more of these tales: and while perhaps harder than ever we maintained our high standard of low fun we were treated to discourses on two subjects that I seemed to have heard before and lay very much on Eve's mind: first, that she was born out of her century, that she belonged to slower and sweeter times: and secondly that if she had her way all the white civilizers would be returned to their own countries, or drowned, and the simple *natural* natives allowed to go their own *simple* and natural ways—and she'd do it *today* if *she* was in power.

It must have been about the fourth day, when we were beginning to be weary of our high time, that someone in the bar mentioned Aphrodisium. The ruins of a Roman pleasure resort, a desert shrine for the rites of Venus. It sounded provocative, we had not yet driven into the desert—and with relief we fell on the idea and began to bargain for a car to take us there the next day.

We set out early in a big old saloon—Harry, Roddy and I. Eve felt too tired, she wanted to enjoy a day of rest without us. We drove out through the dry cactus-lined road, past the large last villas and their palm-lined gardens—and then the road ran straight for miles through flat grey-buff scrubby sand. A desolate place like a dried-up marsh, with sea away on one side and a line of lion-coloured hills far ahead. Occasionally we met a car or a camel. The only people we saw were groups of isolated Bedouins, tattooed and always dressed blue—the nomadic poor who stored up sometimes such great riches.

We came to the hills and turned off onto a track of sharp stones and clay. And then up the side of a hill was Aphrodisium—now no more than a single triumphal arch, the remains of a piscine and the foundations of brothels. It was nothing much: but that one great arch standing alone in the desert, framing always a lonely vista, yet with no direction, with no back nor front, simply a great decorated arch—that arch dwarfed the desert with a splendid gravity it never possessed in the days of ancient pleasure.

It was a long day. When at about six we returned, Eve had gone.

It happened that the moment we entered the hotel the woman at the desk asked in polite greeting: 'And Madame's car arrived all right?'

'Madame's car?'

'You have not seen Madame? Ah!'

'What do you mean? What car?'

'The car Madame hired for Aphrodisium.'

'Oh—what a confounded nuisance!'

It seemed just a nuisance, for Eve and for us; and

also because of that feeling of insecurity that comes when coincidence happens but does not take effect. (You were there? Why, *we* were all there at the time!)

But Harry was worried. Tunis, the Woman of North Africa, is a soft place. But there is still highway robbery, and there is still not much love lost by the Arab for his white protector. A white woman is safe with a good Moslem, she is of no interest to him; but not all Moslems are good. And above all one cannot quite divorce the idea of the desert from its old adventurous rôle: just as it is not easy to walk alone in an Arab village at night without wondering . . . without looking too carefully at that shadowed doorway, at this shape by the wall. . . .

To Harry's mind there rose the idea of a search party. We tried to dissuade him—it was not yet even dark: but he insisted at least on enquiring from whom she had obtained the car, and who the driver was. We were directed first to one house and then to another by the Arab willingness to provide pleasure first and accuracy last. We went to every place where a car could have been hired—there were about four—and none of them had been approached by Eve.

'Perhaps,' I found it difficult to say, 'she hasn't gone at all. Perhaps it's—well, one of her things.'

Harry looked sour. He looked uncertain too.

'What the hell's one to do?'

'Wait at least an hour—until sundown.'

'But supposing—'

He stood there furrowing his brow: strong, capable —but undecided. He half believed this was one of Eve's romantic tricks—he had noticed their reappearance during the last days—but he did not *know*. It was possible something else had happened, it was the weathered fable 'Wolf! Wolf!' and how truly appalling that story can be I only realized fully that day. For as the story goes it takes no account of the feelings of those who love the boy who is finally consumed by the wolf—and Harry was in love with Eve, and as there remained a small possibility of the danger being real he was drawn to protect her. The beloved liar can play indefinitely with the feelings of the lover: the only definition lies in the lover's final exhaustion, but by that time he has ceased to love.

However, we got him back to the hotel for a time. Roddy and I ordered drinks, Harry refused—he wanted to keep a clear head. We considered all the alternatives. 'She might have got a lift on a jeep,' I remember saying indecisively for want of something to say, 'or a lorry.'

'If you ask me,' Roddy surveyed gravely his cigarette tip, 'there's a ship in the desert. Few could penetrate the eye of a needle in such a haystack without the help of a camel.'

He got no response. Harry turned away and went to talk to the lady at the desk. It appeared that Eve had made quite a fuss about her expedition. The lady laughed at how unbelievable the English were, you would have thought Madame was about to cross the Sahara itself. But, the lady said—conspiring politely and amusedly with us—she herself kept quiet and allowed Madame to have her amusement. She was sure she would be back soon. When we said that no car had been hired, she was surprised—politely surprised. And politely she suggested all the alternatives we had already talked of, shaking her head in polite astonishment but not impressed; for her it was no more extraordinary than a wrong turning taken in a London street.

It was a dreadful half-hour, blankly dreadful because we could do nothing, actively dreadful because Harry was stoking up his anxiety. Finally he phoned the police. It so happened that the officer was just then on his way to the hotel for an aperitif. He would discuss the matter immediately.

He was tough, leathery, and attentive. I remember wondering how he kept cool in such a uniform. He finished his aperitif at his ease, then asked us to wait one moment. The bar adjoined the street, we were sitting by the alcove windows and the jasmin-sellers could stretch their hands up to us. Already they had begun their evening seduction. The officer watched the street for a minute, then beckoned to a passing Arab. He spoke a few sentences in Arabic. The Arab pointed down the road and smiling nodded. The officer turned to us and said:

'Madame Camberley went to the station this morning and took a train for Tunis.'

'Tunis!'

'Certainly. Everybody knows this. But if it will make you happier I will have the station telephoned, you can speak with them yourselves. . . .'

It appeared that all this time a hundred people passing up and down the road could have told us this. Events of this kind were bush-telegraphed from man to man as ordinary news of the day: little went unknown in that small town, it was possible to know where everyone was from half-hour to half-hour—in what café, in what house, at the station. The French lady at the desk had not made the effort of so simple an enquiry either from torpor, or perhaps from the necessity of remaining where she was: and with the Arabs we had seen about the hiring of a car—in their case it had been a question of a desire to please by answering our question, not of giving other information which probably for any number of reasons we might already know.

It was exasperating. But we were relieved. Tunis was only an hour or more away by train; and why shouldn't she feel bored alone and go in for some—shopping?

Harry shook his head and reluctantly, admiringly at last, grinned: 'Extraordinary. When you think how frightened she was at the beginning—and now! Off on a train alone in darkest Africa!'

Then the look of alarm again. 'But still—is she all right? She's damned late.'

'These trains.'

'If she's missed the last,' Roddy said, 'she'll get a nice clean room at the Hôtel de la Gare et de la Poste et de la France et de l'Univers *et* de Carthage.'

Then, no more than a few minutes after we had heard what previously we could have heard so easily, the telegram came. It was given to Harry. He read it. I saw his mouth grow angry, then he controlled himself, he only gave a click with his tongue and handed the piece of paper to us.

GOOD NOT STANDIT FLEW BACK WAITING HOTEL PLEASE STAY WRITING LOVE EEV.

'Good not' became 'could not' and while Roddy told Harry that it was after all understandable—in

spite of the heat and the flies, and in spite of the
affirmative idyll of the place, a woman might want to
get back to her clothes, you cannot tell how serious
that might be—while thus they simmered it down, I
alone suffered the full dark apprehension of the phrase
'Could not stand it'. With her letter the storm would
break.

Jasmin Jasmin throatily echoed: and to drive those
boys away we each bought a posy and sat there holding
them, whites holding white buds, three with buds and
thoughts. It is not unusual for a man to hold jasmin
buds in Tunis, but it felt unusual for us.

It takes some time to receive a letter in Tunisia.
There is a well-staffed postal service that smells of hot
metal; but it travels at its own speed, it contains its
own time. So that the next day and the day after we
still sat holding buds. Sometimes we held them there
in our hands, sometimes we held them figuratively.
It was in the evening that clusters of white buds were
there: and in the day there were black buds of flies—
only those flies were not quite black because of their
cream bodies. When one is thinking and has nothing
to do, one sits clutched like a statue and there is endless time to watch hands, buds and flies.

Outwardly there was little to worry about. An adult
had simply decided to leave—for reasons of her own
that were to be sensibly defined in a letter, reasons
presumably of heat or tedium—and she had left by
safe aeroplane to a known destination where her
luggage was: it might even, on the surface, have been
hailed by an objective observer as a glorious move—
showing new initiative where before there had been
little, and showing good consideration for others in

arrangements made for a telegram, a letter, and a request to those left to stay as long as they wished. But while outwardly no cause showed for anxiety, each of us, while holding similar buds, had special anxieties of his own.

Mine were centred round the words 'couldn't stand it'. I simply feared the arrival of that letter—even then on its way—and all it would bring. Roddy was made anxious by boredom. He had to keep quiet, the high spirit of our facetion was over, no longer did we laugh at his jokes and mild fooling: with the position reversed, with Eve to entertain, he might have managed, but without the artificial stimulus of drink or some other particular he could never really feel at home with Harry. But of course it was Harry who contributed most to our separate anxieties—he must simply have felt, I'm sure against his will, that it was *wrong* for her to have left so suddenly. Why it was wrong could not sensibly be argued: nor did he try. But wrong it was—unfamiliar, unwifely, uneasy.

Once he exploded: 'What's gone wrong with this damned holiday?'

But no-one answered. We might have blamed the heat or the flies—I forget—but he got no answer to his question because there was none, nor did he expect one.

Then one day the letter came. I saw it lying in the pigeon-hole above Harry's key. A letter can lie flat in those holes—thin, addressless, anonymous: a very different matter to the letter in one's hands. So my hands asked for that letter, I would see M. Camberley in a minute—and then it was in my pocket, even then more presenceful than the moment in my hands when

I made sure of its postmark and its large, back-sloped handwriting. It was nearly lunchtime, Harry would soon be coming back from a bathe—for apart from holding our buds we did walk about a little and bathe in the sultry, grey-blue sea—and I walked out onto the verandah to wait. I knew that really I must give him the letter.

But as the Mexicans passed on their honking burros beneath, as the pale-eyed dogs slunk about and lumps of cream-coloured wool containing women hurried on their faceless way—I could not help thinking how this was the end of Eve's life of illusion. How she had craved against reality, even in the first of our days on that romantic littoral of France—and that only love had completed that romance, dissolving her old wish for illusion and, as love does, producing in fact another and a stronger fantasy. And I wondered again back to us three men, and how again with our three different minds we had assessed Eve's first spirit of illusion: Roddy must have liked it because he could neither stand too much reality nor too much fantasy— he liked a change, and I suppose Eve's personality gave this: Harry liked, or at least condoned it, because he was in a state of husband-protector, and her silly stories, after he had learned not to take them too seriously, made her seem 'such a little girl': and as for myself—such a facility for mixing reality and illusion was a curiosity, and in any case I have never found a really satisfactory argument for the one or the other, nor any real test for distinguishing between them.

Harry came back, and while he was changing I still kept the letter in my pocket. We went down to lunch, and found Roddy already arguing with the black Sudanese waiter over the menu.

'We're going to have,' he said, 'kus-kus for a change.'

We sat down and I said as casually as I could: 'By the way, Harry—a letter. I think it's from Eve.'

'Good.'

He took it and broke it open. I felt it should have been slit open very slowly with a long precise paper-knife.

I tried not to watch his face. When I did it showed no emotion, he wore again with gruff consideration that invisible overcoat.

Suddenly he grunted. 'Well—of all the . . .' he said. Then he made a blowing sniff—a sinus sound, a noise of rebuke.

I found myself so controlled that, as it were placing the tips of my fingers together, I came out with a phrase honoured by time in novels of detection: 'Nothing wrong I hope?'

He did not answer. Then looked up as if he had just heard. 'No, nothing much.'

He looked round the restaurant as if he were examining it for the first time. But it was for the last time. Now he exploded: 'Hell, I'm going back. I'm sick of this.'

I pretended to look surprised.

Roddy murmured in one of his voices: 'This is so sudden, Mr. Camberley.'

Harry tossed me the letter.

It was quite a long letter—I cannot hope to reproduce it here. But it said in fact that she had not been able to stand the heat and the flies and what she called the 'breathlessness' of the place, she felt she couldn't breathe and on an impulse had gone into Tunis in the hope of a plane. It had come over her all of a sudden, it was like being stifled by a pillow. She was very sorry if she had disturbed things—but she knew he'd understand. She simply couldn't help it. But now she was all right, it was fine being back at the hotel— how cool and clear it felt. Then there followed a little about new people who had arrived, and it ended with a little love, which, since Harry was watching me, I made an obtrusive act of skipping.

He saw this, and grunted:

'The P.S.'

The P.S. said she hardly dared to tell him, but there had been no seat on any regular plane, and she had managed to go shares with a married couple in hiring a private plane.

'Hell,' said Harry, 'we're not as well off as *that*.'

That afternoon we telephoned for seats on the evening plane, packed and took the train to Tunis. We felt a little brighter, a movement was being made: but it was not such a happy train as the one we had come by. I remember it distinguished only by un- repeatable talk of hours of destination and whether we should stay a night in Marseilles or not, by an old brass sign beneath the window, half-erased, which read: 'Pour bien relever la glace . . . vitellement mais sans brutalité,' and by the magnificent entrance into the carriage of a huge Arab father dressed in fine silk and holding proudly the hand of his little son, while three women—Liquorice-All-Sorts with beautifully kohled eyes—followed obediently behind. How much simpler if Eve had been born an Arab woman . . .

We had a long time to hang about in Tunis. The

plane was delayed. We went and had coffee at the slave-market in the Souks, we looked moodily over the stagnant green water that laked its way towards Carthage, we had more coffee in a French-colonial avenue lined with purple acacia-like trees. The sound of a Jewish feast tinkled its silver-bell music from a laughing window above, an old Mexican-hat drove an ancient black growler pulled by two mauve-and-white marbled horses, many ragged children begged from us and the little white-canopied trams clanged past and at last it was time to leave.

Then we said goodbye to Roddy, who was off to Kairouan, and after another long wait for the airbus whose driver could not be found, and a longer wait while the airplane was tinkered with, we lurched horribly off the ground and into the night.

XV

IT was a clear night, even at our small altitude the stars seemed nearer, and below against the indigo of air and sea the clouds extended flat like a land of white snow.

I had time and leisure to consider why I was going back. Was this prompted by those close, remote feelings of friendship for Harry? Or by affection for Eve? Or by a less selfish sense of duty as mediator, simply to fulfil the need of a third person around in case of trouble? Or more simply to escape the flies and return to my manuscripts in the hotel? I shall never know. According to my mood I can choose as the truth one or the other: but to know, never.

It was impossible not to be pleased by Marseilles. First, one was relieved by a safe landing. Then for once—probably because we were already late—the formalities were hurried through and the airbus was ready and swift. Then even the Canebière felt cool and orderly after the confusions of Tunis. We dined well off food more acceptable to our habitual palates, and quite cheerfully we went to a few bars. It was, too, a relief to be away from Roddy, we could talk easily now on common ground. We found a couple of girls and danced a lot. Harry did not take the opportunity of having a little serious fun on the side.

When we arrived at the hotel along the coast the next afternoon, it was to find that Madame was out shopping. And, like a dove of white peace, there was the expected letter recalling Harry to his office. It had only arrived that morning, he was not late for it. But he knew that without argument at all he must drive north the next day. I remember very clearly how I saw that letter as a dove of peace. It could indeed have suggested the opposite—war, a red show-down. But I must have been reminded of the other letter, Eve's to Tunis, and apart from its whole lie the inspired emphasis on her being stifled. For she had arisen into detail. I am sure that if she had been talking with us, and had not been controlled by her pen, she would have made a much longer story of it. It showed that she could use her romantic lying to purpose. She could use her habit, ruthlessly it seemed, to achieve her ends. The innocence of that romantic facility was soiled—but it showed also a decision to remain within the framework of her marriage: Eve had either not the strength, or not the courage (or not a strong enough wish?) to burst the conventions. It seemed that she would contain her feelings and leave the next day without argument.

It really was remarkably cool on the hotel terrace—that is, it was as warm as ever but so much clearer than on the African coast. I found myself enjoying all those neatnesses that previously I had despised: and what had once seemed fantastic became usual after the greater fantasy, the near-insanity of Tunisia. The pedal-boats lay beached in a neat row, the sea sparkled merrily after the sultry monster we had known, the edges of the roads were cleanly defined, the people came and went and one knew what their purpose might be. All was again comprehensible. Even when

I picked up the paper and read a chance item about a collision in a taxi.

'. . . un voyageur eut la langue coupée. Le medecin de l'assurance, examinant la langue amputée, trouva la trace d'une dent étrangère. Une enquête fut faite. Le voyageur n'était pas seul dans le taxi. Il était en train d'embrasser une dame quand l'accident avait eu lieu. La compagnie soutient que la forme de la blessure indiquait que le passager eu la langue coupée par les dents de cette dame. L'imprudence du voyageur fut admise par le tribunal et l'indemnité fut reduite au quart de ce qu'elle eût pu être si le blessé s'était mordu lui-même.'

Even then I could look up with only a simple flinch and resume the scene before me with equanimity.

At six-thirty Eve came home flushed and breathless. She had been hurrying.

'Why! You here already?'

We had telegraphed that we would arrive during the afternoon.

'I had no idea . . .!' she went on, and then we all greeted each other and asked each other how we'd been? Harry was overjoyed to see her, and it seemed that genuinely she was pleased to see him.

After these effervescences we quietened and sighed saying nothing. Then Harry pulled a long face: 'Well Eve, it's all over. I've had a missive from the company. Tomorrow we take the high road.'

'The high road?'

'Home. Got to. No question.'

She looked bewildered. She suddenly lost poise, she looked smaller.

'Oh.'

'Co-ome on old thing! All good things have to come to an end.'

'I know.'

'And anyway, we've got no money left.'

'Money?'

'When some of us go traipsing about darkest Africa in private airplanes . . .' Harry was smiling, turning on all joviality to stiffen the troops, a parent on the last day of holiday.

'Oh Harry, I couldn't help that, really I couldn't.'

'Now now now. I'm not taking umbrage. Simply a fact. No more of the necessary, darling.' He opened his hands wide.

Eve gave a little smile, her head went on one side, considering. Then she took a breath.

'Couldn't you . . .' she started then stopped. I held my breath.

Then she suddenly pointed at me.

'What about him?'

My held breath came instantly loose. 'I'm broke too,' I said in a voice that should have rung despair but must have sounded most enthusiastic: 'I've got to go north too.'

Eve looked at me for a moment of steel suspicion—then sighed. She seemed to relax, she almost yawned and said: 'Well—that's *that* then.'

Suddenly, almost naturally, she jerked herself together, clapped a hand to her forehead and said: 'Damn!'

We waited.

'Damn, I'll have to go into the town again. Something I ordered. I'll have to pick it up.'

'We could pass in the morning?' Harry suggested.

'No, better make sure.'

'What is it?'

'Oh . . . something.'

'Well, we'll come in with you. The car's outside.'

There was hardly a pause before Eve pouted and made a motherly face at Harry, cooing: 'No, darling! After all that long drive from nasty Marseilles you're tired. You—just—stay—here—and—rest.'

'But we've been sitting here hours.'

'You—stay—here. I simply wouldn't *dream* of it. Waiter!'

Harry was looking at her half shrewd, half amused.

'Waiter,' Eve called regally, 'two pernods for these two gentlemen.' She had already gathered herself and was moving. 'I shan't be long,' she called.

Harry watched her go. 'Well, thank God, she doesn't seem too put out.'

'No,' I said. Then: 'Here's mud in your eye!'

A silly phrase—I regretted it immediately. That regret, and a long silence from Harry, started me thinking: What if, all the time, he really knew? I glanced privately at him—and what I saw only confirmed the possibility. There he sat, his strong square overcoat of a face expressing nothing but a normal gravity. How could one know what such a man thought? However much he might be limited, Harry had a certain experience of life and he had his ethical values. It was only difficult for him to express these. He was a reserved Englishman, and that reservation had grown into his tongue. It was, in fact, possible that he knew. And that patiently he had decided to do nothing about

it either for fear of losing Eve; or even in a painful
moment of understanding that indiscretions can erupt
in the most ordered lives, and that they must gently be
purged and forgiven. All this was possible—and the
one certainty was that he would never have said a
word about it to me. Among the multiple reasons for
an Englishman's reserve is fear of failure, fear of
ridicule. Quite apart from his home, an Englishman
is his own castle.

I tried to dismiss this new and most disturbing train
of thought—among other things he would know I
knew—but I could not thoroughly convince myself.
At length we had another drink and started talking
about the journey back. An hour passed, and still Eve
had not returned.

Harry looked once or twice at his watch.

'I hope I shan't have to go and look for her,' he
said. What did that mean?

I said: 'Let's wash for dinner.'

Then there she was. She came forward unsmiling
with her chin set.

'I know, I know, I *know*—I've been a long time.
Well, I couldn't help it.'

It was very awkward. We waited—both unsure. I
felt the storm breaking. Now. But now she suddenly
broke out laughing and tossed Harry a parcel. She
went to him and hugged him round his neck. 'Present
for a good boy! Souvenir de la France!'

And Harry unwrapped the paper from around a
large bottle of something called "Cylindre". Gentlemen's Toilet Lotion.

'Well!' said Harry and he sat back looking amazed.
'Goodness me!' he said.

My pernod went down the wrong way, and I can only remember coughing till the world was black.

We drove north the next morning. Eve was much quieter. Once or twice I saw her looking at Harry curiously—her head only half towards him in the front seat, as people might half-look at a strange neighbour in the cinema.

Her performance the previous evening must have cost an effort. Try as I might, I could not find her hard. I do not think it had been easy for her. She had been in a fix, she had to get out and say her goodbye to that man, and she had to return with a parcel. The only extraordinary part of it was her choice of that particular purchase: but this was perhaps no more than another example of an always surprising feminine phenomenon —the great practical streak that accompanies what might seem a greatly illogical mind. Had the position been reversed, had she been a man, I could see her coming back with some wild blunder—an ashtray, a pink rabbit.

Besides, she had not thrown Harry off for this lover. She was in a dangerous predicament—but she had not faced an exact choice. We have our instinct for pre-servation—emotion does not necessarily bubble a life right over. I think Eve had her share of hopeful cunning: she was prepared to wait a little, and hoped somehow —as a schoolgirl might—to worm her way out of it. She hated confession.

Our drive north was eventless—if I omit what are the greatest events, for we were driving from summer into autumn, our little machine was changing the seasons for us. How clear and clean the air became, what fogs and frost the mind predicted! The angles of the light were changed, leaves blew free, red roofs changed to blue, the north was opening up for another of its brisk jewelled seasons. It was a most eventful drive.

And for myself there lay ahead, I meanly rejoiced, an extra freedom. For now those two must go back to Oxley: and I must resume in London my separate life. No more superintention. As we crossed the Seine by the Pont Royal, there came clattering under the great wall of the Louvre a detachment of cuirassiers. They rode squat horses, they were thickset men themselves, their plumes swung with menace from brassy helmets, their boots and their sabres gave them an inelegant look of business. I did not connect this sudden appearance with anything at the time—there was only an undefined feeling of uneasiness.

And time must again be allowed to pass. I did not go down to Oxley for a full year or more. The freshness of autumn brought a desire for work, and to settle down for a few months' quiet among plants and books. However, at one time or another, among all else that went on, I chanced to see a little of them.

Roddy Meredith came back from the south in late October, brown and broke. Kairouan had been wonderful; it had been considerably pretty: then he had gone further south and had fallen in with some rather important Arabs who had invited him as guest of honour to some grand pavilioned banquet. The honey-baked sheep had been placed before him and in time he had been offered the honoured eye, which with rather shady aplomb he had managed to swallow— a step, but only a short step, he said, better than eating boiled cod gills with a Viking chief in Stavanger. But Roddy was not happy to be back. He had no feeling for work, and though perhaps the fringe of London's little season might have tempted him, he would have preferred heartily to continue the southern indolences. However, in the sad state of a penniless dilettante, he had to live—and live quite well—and he now threw himself with animation into a fashionable hunt for the more grotesque furnitures of the 'Twenties—cubist cushions with long Turkish tassels, great sideboards of smouldering glass, oxidized fires whirling electric logs.

When he told me this, I remembered some of the stuff at "Uplands"—and told him of some of the small marvels of Harry's marine furniture. Roddy wondered whether society was really yet ready for this—then he wondered back to Eve and Harry and began to pump me as to what had really been in the air.

'Nothing I know of.'

He glanced at me. 'You *are* a simple fellow.'

'Eh?'

'You're the worst liar I've *ever* met. Remove your eyes from mine—I know that frank blank stare. And look at your arms—one to either side, chest bravely exposed . . . slump back again, fidget with something as you usually do when you're telling the truth. You've really no *idea*?'

I think then I must have begun to fidget a lot—for he began to laugh while I said: 'You know very well about Eve's life of fancy. The reality unsettled her. It's never very nice to wake from a pleasant dream.

You find that the only person who's woken up is your dear old self—and however much you like yourself, you're never quite as good as in your pleasant dream. Eve was at first stunned by the actuality of blue seas and mimosa and so forth . . . then she had to admit who was looking at the mimosa, who but her dear old self, the same bundle of unfulfilled desires. She had to find discontent. God knows what she dreamed up—an iceberg, a bit of Baffinland, a night with the boys on Spitsbergen. Or at least, we do have an idea what she dreamed up—remember that talk about living in another century? Diddled by space, she took to time.'

Roddy gave quite a hearty snort:

'Excellent. You've yet to learn that Eve is a woman.'

'And you mean by that?'

'Have you ever met a *really* romantic woman?'

'Of course I have.'

'Have you seen, say, one of your really romantic women overcome by the still beauty of a lake with a moon above like a flying saucer—then seen her suddenly catch sight of her reflection in the very water and moonlight whose stillness and magic overcame her?'

'Yes. And she pats her hair! But quite rightly too—because she feels herself part of the romance.'

'And that is exactly unromantic. She'll never let beauty alone, but wants to build a house in it. With plenty of cupboard space too.'

'I've met many who cordially dislike cupboard space.'

'All right yes. There are some. But be fair—the majority . . .'

'You're biassed,' I said.

'And you're knocked up with lust.'

'In any case—that word "majority". I don't like talking generalities. And Eve's no ordinary woman.'

'Ah-ha!'

'Ah-ha to you back. And pooey on you too.'

'Then suppose Eve's a particular,' Roddy said, 'and suppose I repeat that I do *not* happen to be knocked up by your own moribund lust—yes, I know that Eve is a particular of your own, too, I've seen you at it, drooling away like a bloody Newfoundland—'

'I say, old man . . .'

'Suppose Eve is an unusual woman, which I don't really think, and suppose I can see her more clearly than you, which is inevitable . . . take my word for it, that little one's a lot tougher than you think.'

'You mean she's a capable woman when necessary.'

'I mean her fantasies are impure. She's not necessarily swept away. At a whim she can ground them for her own practical purposes. Her dreams are the stuff taps are made of.'

'It's six o'clock, I must go.'

He sniggered, and I accused him of presenting a fait accompli without proof—but I was in a hurry to be away. It was uncomfortable to argue against what I knew to be true. Or perhaps what I felt to be half-true—for the matter of Eve's conduct had not yet been resolved.

A month later I saw her.

Husbands may be locked up in offices, but writers can infest the streets. And opposite the air terminus in Buckingham Palace Road there is a public library at whose door often in those weeks I smoked away the time from the large and heavy books inside. One day Eve passed.

She passed hurrying straight along—one moment framed in the door and then quickly gone. I went forward to call to her—then stopped myself, feeling again the danger of becoming involved in heaven knows what: it seemed impossible to speak to Eve without some emotional upset. I saw her cross the road and make for the air terminus. Then, irritated by my own caution, and the next moment excusing that irritation by a sudden rational taste for a cup of tea—and omitting to imagine why most probably she might wish to visit an air office—I jabbed down my cigarette and went after her.

When I entered the hall she was greeting the garage-man, her pilot, her Georges. And this time just as I saw them they saw me. Eve looked surprised, she made a little gesture, a move forward at me. I did not notice Georges' expression for already I was waving—waving and hurrying fast away. It was meant to be a casual wave, a busy but genial wave: I expect it looked more like the winnowing of an idiot wreathed in smiles and invisible flags. I've often wondered what she thought.

Then in December Harry telephoned to ask me if I could meet him for a late supper. Something he had to tell me, something to celebrate: he seemed in high spirits.

It was a chill, damp night with a magic of fog about. I was a little early at the night-club where we had arranged to meet, and sat for some time in the vestibule tasting the warmth, a slow drink, and the first movements of guests arriving to stir up a glitter of night. A beating of drums sounded somewhere along a passage that muffled what music was being played. Harry came in at about midnight: trust a man who looks like an overcoat advertisement to wear over his dinner jacket a khaki mackintosh covered with leather buttons.

'Ha!' he said when he saw me. He gave that mackintosh to a man who pretended not to see it, and came over.

'Shall we wend our way?'

We entered the smokeless darklit room and the drums revealed their chatter of music. Few people yet. We chose a table against the wall where we could talk. Then we chose a bottle of whisky with which to talk, and I suppose I started by asking him what a married man was doing alone in the night so far from home.

'Bolivians,' he said. 'Propellers for Bolivians. And they haven't even got a sea. Lake stuff.'

'Indeed!'

'As a matter of fact, I ought to be with them now. Wine-ing and dining. Gave them the slip. Hope they don't decide to propel their good selves in this direction —I took the precaution of dropping them home.'

'And Mrs. Camberley?'

'At home. Martie's gone to stay the night with her—remember Martie?'

'Of course. Well, you seem to have tied that up neatly.'

'By the by—there's romance in the air!'

'Oh.'

222

'Ay. Sex has reared its ugly head.'

'Have another drink?'

'Thanking you kindly.'

I looked round: 'Not very full tonight, is it?'

'Early yet. Fill up later.'

He looked deeply into his glass. 'Ay,' he grunted. 'Sex. No keeping a good girl down.'

'Ah, here's another party. Quite a tableful. That woman in the blue dress—'

'That Martie! D'you remember old Barney Barnett —chap played the piano? Well, she's hooked him. Good and proper. Sold him a pup and hooked him.'

'Gracious!'

'Line and sinker, old man. Bit of a flutter down there I can tell you.'

'You do have a time at Oxley.'

'Do we not?'

We watched while the club filled. Harry sat glowing goodwill, reddening with it. Now the music seldom ceased, the shapes of things were softened by smoke and by alcohol and by music and by the emanations of many people: where the light struck there was a glitter from the women's dresses and their jewelry, and a smooth bland shine came from their pale shoulders and the white starched shirts of the men. Where there was no light the room stretched dark with tables, with the sense of moving shapes, with comforting recessive darkness—and this dark was echoed by the black evening clothes of the men and the big black piano and black dais-curtain framing the band.

There was an air of comfort and excited well-being. Harry sat back pleased—a different look on his face

to the one that had smugged him in that dancing bar
in Marseilles. Here all was well. And I felt this too—
I have always suspected those writers who find only
apathy and ill in the night-clubs they so easily people
with white masks. I think most people I have seen in
night-clubs have been laughing, full of blood and life,
out for a night's good time and as merry as a good
time should be. And by merry I do not necessarily
mean 'charmingly gay'.

Later I remembered Harry's talk of a celebration.
'By the way—you haven't told me yet . . . what . . .?'

He had been waiting. 'What this is in aid of?' he
said quickly.

I nodded and gave him a great piercing look to egg
him on.

He grew pretentiously grave, he seemed to swell.
Then he laughed, and grew grave again:

'I am about to become a father!' he said.

'Good God! I mean . . . congratulations . . .'

We solemnly raised our glasses.

'To Dad!'

'To the future Mister Camberley!'

When that was done I searched for words:

'And how many months gone is . . . I mean, *when*
is Eve going to . . .?'

'April.'

The best thing then to do was to raise our glasses
again. Desperately I tried not to count back the
months, desperately I counted. I kept miscounting, I
suppose in an attempt to fix it right for Harry; and at
length—because we began gabbling hard about sons
and boys and our own boyhood and ourselves—gave
it up.

THE FACE OF INNOCENCE

We had a boisterous evening and did not part until the club closed very much later. I can remember looking at Harry now and then and wondering whether after all he did know or whether not; and thinking that in any case, either from subterfuge or from natural pride, he would cause a celebration: but what conclusion I came to remains lost in the fog.

On the 23rd of April of the following year a son was born to Eve. Telegrams were exchanged. Both did well.

XVI

IT has been insisted that it never rains but it pours—though of course really it rains a little most of the time. However, I cannot help admitting it seemed to pour the next time I visited "Uplands". It was to meet the new Miles George Camberley.

A week before, on a misty morning in early September, a morning out of season, cold and strange—ghosts appeared in the Park. The Serpentine lay out of sight, perhaps the mist came from that calm water—but out before the trees on the open field guns thundered, harness jingled, sharp cries of command cut the air as busbies and horses appeared and vanished in the still white mist. It seemed that Waterloo was being fought again. It was the Royal Horse Artillery in their full hussarish uniform firing an occasional salute. Blue elegance, yellow frogging, a flash of red and silver—it was a moving sight, for nothing modern spoiled the illusion, and the mist made a memorable frame. As must henceforth be my lot, the appearance of mounted soldiers in the Park held a significance of loyalties, and I was back to that conversation with Roddy of so long ago when once the Horse Guards passed : and so when a day or two later Harry Camberley telephoned to ask me down to see the new baby I was in no mood to refuse.

Although I adore some children, I do not very much like babies. Most of them look to me like Hinden-

burg. It is not so easy to differentiate between them as
people suggest—'he's got his father's nose, his mother's
eyes' seems too often confected. It is plain enough that
the miniature fingers and toes and other parts have the
precise appeal of the miniature: but is that enough?
Possibly I was frightened once by a very nasty baby
in the woodshed.

Still—there babies are, and now I must go back a
bit on my words to say that little Miles in the pram
in his white ski-bonnet did not look at all like Hinden-
burg. With his high cheekbones and his brown eyes
and his wet black hair he looked most Gallic.

Eve stood a little away while Harry and I bent over
the pram. It was a day of dull low cloud—windless, a
kind of English mistral where the mind is weighed
with pressure and tempers are ruffled by the very
no-wind—and against the dull brick and the black
pram Miles successfully shone: his white clothes shone,
his flesh gleamed its freshness, and I saw a fatherly
amused wonder shining back from Harry's eyes. No,
I do not think he knew. It may be possible, if instead
he did know, that a sense of possession and a warm
feeling for protection might have brought such life
to a husband's eye. But from that moment, and from
noticing other small actions of his during the day, I
feel pretty sure he knew nothing.

Eve stood to one side, pretending to busy herself
with a plastic rattle-and-bell-and-twinkle machine:
she stood aside with that shocking unconcern that
mothers show for their children—the unconcern that
shows when without batting an eyelid they hand their
children to complete strangers to rock and diddle.
Yet now and again I caught her watching us. She

watched wisely, slowly, carefully. I always think that
even if one does not care much for babies one ought
to go through some of the motions of caring—babies
do seem to carry an importance in the lives of their
parents—and I was shuffling about the pram and
making quite a few different noises. But of course
thinking of other things. Of Harry, and of Eve's unconcern. I had seen the same unconcern a dozen times
before—and of course it is really a kind of pleased
mask. But I am afraid that nevertheless suspicions still
arose—was there in Eve, despite the instincts of mother-
hood, a conflicting shame? Or a conflicting embarrassment that this was not where the child should be? Or
even—and it was possible—with some part of her
divided mind, with that part that lived a life of self
walled against the real world, had she developed in
spite of all the good and practical sides to her nature
a deep apathy—the sad selfishness of a woman who
cannot care for her child?

But a little later she was adjusting the sunshade of
the pram against the dark light from those low clouds,
a vexed frown of concentration on her forehead as her
fingers fiddled a little metal wing-nut.

We went outside. I had brought Roddy down,
remembering his new interest in new-old furnishings.
He too had been introduced to the baby. Ill-at-ease,
he too had tried. But his methods were slicker and
more ruthless than mine. He had said it had its mother's
toes and it looked as brown as a fiddle, and a little
more like that—and off he wandered, having done
quite well; but, I was glad to see, tripping himself
with the elementary error of labelling the little man
'it'. Now he was standing in the 'lounge' engrossed

with a real child of Harry's—that brass ship's engine-room telegraph made into a cigar-cutter.

We lunched and the afternoon began.

It was still as dull, and I think this dullness had begun by then to ruffle all our minds. At all events, when at two-thirty we were finished, one had the feeling that there was nothing to do—the country looked uninviting for a walk—yet more than anything one wanted action. It was not like a day of rain, when most is decided for you: it was indeliberate. I believe Harry felt this as much as anyone, and accordingly braced himself and declared a plan of operation. He did not suggest anything very exciting. But it was something, it was action.

He would take the car over to Martie's house and collect her back to continue bottling the plums. Martie's own car had broken down, Martie was kindly bottling their plums for them at "Uplands". Besides, now he came to think of it, she had suggested coming that very afternoon—because Mr. Barnett was proposing to visit her.

'She's a bit flustered you know,' Harry laughed. 'She doesn't think it quite right for the two of them to be alone together in the house.'

So it was hands up those who want a drive? He looked from Roddy to me and back bright-eyed, anxious to give us a treat. Roddy looked at that ship's telegraph, winced, and put his hand up. Had it been a laliquely elephant smoking a shagreen cigarette holder, nothing would have moved him. Now anything would, fashion is a funny thing.

Eve of course could not leave the baby. I had as little wish for a ride in a car as a walk, and said I would stay and look around the garden: in any case it would be rather a crush coming back, five people and all that.

Off they crunched down the gravel drive. Eve took the baby upstairs. There was silence. I walked out of that stonily stippled, austerely gadgeted room into the garden with its dark-grey clouds. No wind, no light, not a sound. No-one even bothered to hammer on such a day, even the michaelmas daisies had ceased their sad mauve shine. I mooched, I remember walking up to a tool-shed, creosoted and locked, a dead look in its one blind window that reflected nothing. Then I remember the words coming to my lips: 'Goodbye summer, summer goodbye . . .' but stopped them quickly, for that is a song that is said to be dangerous to sing.

I turned back to the house and saw Eve was standing there.

Pale against the darkness of the room behind, she made a slight wave of her hand. 'Baby's asleep,' she murmured when I joined her.

For a few moments we stood there in silence. I wanted to break it. Words kept coming to my lips: but they were all too meaningless to speak. I knew she was storing something herself.

Then it came. She suddenly said in a loud quick voice:

'I haven't seen you since the airport.'

'The airport?' Then I remembered. 'No, indeed we haven't.'

'It's a very long time ago. It's months. Long before I had—'

'Months. Why, it must have been October!'

We seemed to be two strangers talking loudvoiced at a party. She wanted to say much more. So I tried to break it:

'And how's what's-his-name—Georges, isn't it?'

She seemed not to hear and went on speaking her own thoughts. Her voice appealed half to me, half to the garden clouds:

'It's been so dreadful all these months. I didn't know what to do. I didn't know whether I ought to tell Harry. I didn't know whether I ought to divorce him and go to Georges with his child. I didn't know how to do it in time. We could have gone away. Then somehow—you know I kept wondering about what his name should be. I kept wondering about his name!'

She made a laughing noise, but then her voice returned:

'You know—I tried not to have him at all. I tried a lot of things. What a time, what a dreadful time I must have given the poor mite. But he stayed. Yes, he wanted to stay . . . and now you see the position.'

She sighed: 'But in a way it's solved. In a way.'

I remember waiting. And then having to ask, as softly as I could: 'How?' And then quickly adding: 'But of course it is.'

She was quiet for a moment. But I saw the rise and fall of her full breasts as she breathed hard on what she remembered.

'I suppose he knows?' I said, knowing it was an absurd question, but somehow to stop that breathing.

'Who?'

'Georges.'

'Oh—him.'

She seemed not interested.

'Why—how is he?'

'I don't know,' she said.

'I don't know and I don't think I want to know,' she went on, turning to me and away from the garden. 'He wanted to leave me, you know. We saw quite a bit of each other when he started flying over first. But then there was another woman. Or he simply got tired and found another woman. I don't blame him. He's not bad. We had our time—and he's a man after all. Or no, that's silly, women get tired too. Anyway, he got tired.

'But then you see I knew I was going to have a baby. And the awful thing was—I tried to keep him. I tried not to let him go for baby's sake. We still used to meet. He did try to be nice. But it was the waiting that was so awful—I waited and waited for him to say something. It was up to him. You'd think I might have said something myself—but no, I never said a word, the baby was my business and yet it could have been his too but that was up to him, that's natural. Oh, how I waited!

'Then one day I knew it was too late. I was very—big. I knew it was too late—and I went straight to him and told him I didn't love him any more and it was all over and goodbye.'

She made that laughing noise again, and now when her eyes looked at me they seemed really amused. Or perhaps they were still astonished: 'Do you know, I've *never* seen a man look so relieved in all my life.'

In the silence that followed I saw what a sad trick had been played on her. I saw that young airman she had first loved—that Erik who had stayed so long a legend of young love, that Erik whom she had seen high above and who had tottered in the sky and had fallen. And now this—this rebirth of the legend, this adult reality who did not die at the height of love but simply cooled off and left her. I saw how toughly this must have hit her romantic mind—and I found myself thinking aloud:

'Poor Eve. You don't seem to have had much luck with your airmen.'

'Air*men*?'

'Oh—nothing. I was just mumbling . . . nothing.'

'No—you said air*men*. What do you mean?'

There was no way out. Or I had not the wit to fabricate one.

'I was just thinking of that old friend of yours, that one years ago—Erik.'

'Oh, Erik.'

She paused. Then she spoke for the first time in a hard voice:

'If you'd like to know, Erik wasn't really an airman. He just liked to go down to the field and look.'

'Oh. Oh well.'

'*And* he seduced me in the front seat of a car, his famous little car parked up a lane. That was how I lost my precious . . . I was so shocked, I left him. I never saw him after. *That*'s my famous Erik.'

I could say nothing. But then a dream came into her voice:

'But I did love him . . . and it could have been wonderful . . .'

Her voice was lost music. It murmured the music we think must come only with middle age—the music, the feeling that often we forget the young have too, music that breaks in our hearts and sings only one refrain: 'All over, all over.' For Eve—yet young, yet beautiful—a part of life had already been over a long time.

I saw she was sobbing. Her breast trembled and the tears quietly slid down her cheeks: 'If only my father . . .' she said loud, clenched between her sobs, head held erect.

'Your father?'

'If only my father were here . . . *he* was wonderful, he was in the war, he was killed. He was a soldier.'

I put my arm round her shoulders. She shook it off savagely. She burst out crying and raved:

'Hell no, he wasn't. I don't know what he was. I never knew him. I don't think my mother knew who he was . . . but if I had, if only I had . . .'

She was laughing loud and crying at the top of her voice. I knew one must slap them or something. I couldn't do it, I raised my hand. . . .

And then as abruptly she stopped, she looked at me terrified, I could see her defences rising like glands in her throat. She hit her hand across her mouth. But through it there came at me, deep with venom hoarsed in a low whisper:

'I *hate* you!'

She turned and ran inside. I heard her sobbing up the stairs and then no more.

It must have been ten minutes later when the sound of the returning car came whirring up the gravel. I know I had recovered a little: enough to face the sounds of people now clattering and talking through the windows. At first I had stood there stunned. But I remember a little later beginning to wonder whether I ought to go up and see her: perhaps hysteria needed help? Then I thought that I could only make it worse —instead of relieving her feelings by confession she had taken the other way, perhaps their very statement had shocked her and the flood could only grow. Best leave her to herself. One small matter consoled me—I had heard no door bang, she must have been sane enough to remember the baby was asleep.

But Harry came in looking anxious. He spoke urgently:

'Everything all right, I suppose?'

I was so astonished I said nothing. He must have been miles away when Eve collapsed.

He saw my frown and a look of fear crossed his face: 'Where's Eve? Where is she?'

'Upstairs resting. She went up a few minutes ago. What on earth's up?'

He sighed. Then he smiled awkwardly and held out an evening paper. 'Of course—you didn't know. Read that. There's a chap loose round here. Armed. Dangerous.'

By that time Martie and the dogs and Roddy and the looming form of Mr. Barnett had crowded in behind and everyone seemed to be speaking at once:

'He's sure to break in somewhere for food!'

'There it is—plain as your life—Oxley Heath!'

'Barney brought us the sad news from London.'

'Nobody told *us*. We might have run him over.'

'Shh. You'll wake the baby!'

Harry became calm and grim. 'Well,' he said, 'don't suppose there's any harm in being prepared.'

He went over to a desk and rummaged round in the

drawers. He came back with a very large revolver from the 1914 War and placed this carefully in the centre of the piano.

'Take a note of that, Mr. Barnett,' Roddy said severely. 'And keep off dem ivories.'

'Oh he wouldn't!' Martie breathed. 'Not at a time like this. Besides—the baby.'

'Play if you like,' Harry said, 'the brat can't hear a thing. Only keep it quiet in case.'

Then he went out into the hall, and while we all settled down more, and the tall dog Peter watched with intelligent incomprehension as Audrey rolled on her back, I heard a clatter of golf-clubs from the hall. Harry brought in four or five sticks and handed one to each of us. 'Never say die,' he said.

And so we laughed—a bit creepily—and sat down to wait in that grim armoury. But nobody took the position very seriously, and Martie said that a nice cup of tea would do us all good. We could call Eve later, when she'd had her rest. And no-one was to move, because she knew where things were and she could get on with her bottling at the same time.

Barney had his black-rimmed spectacles low on his nose, and his weak pale eyes gazed over them at her with wonder. 'Trust the little woman,' he purred, while Martie flushed and went quickly out. 'And inbetweenwhiles yours truly will make bold with the old joanna.' As he sat his great red bulk down he added: 'Upon this festive occasion.'

Harry whispered to me: 'He's simply bowled over by the old girl. Or by her house—here's a photo she's just given him.'

'The Kennels,' Roddy murmured.

I was handed a pale brown photograph of a dark-looking house upright among taller firs. Its façade was covered with beams and pale-brown gravel, and a white wood balcony surmounted the porch.

Barney had begun to sing softly:

> 'Just a little red house
> On a little green hill
> By a wa-ter mill . . .'

I handed the photograph back:

'Not a very red house,' I said.

'Do they have water-mills on hills?' Roddy whispered.

'Only at high water.'

'No really,' Harry said. 'You mustn't. He's being very sweet about her.'

Meanwhile Peter had wandered over to the window and, seeing I suppose no more than the lightless garden under cloud, had sat down to scratch himself. His leg made a thudding noise on the floor. Audrey had stopped rolling and had walked over to Roddy's shoe: she sniffed the toe of this gently for a long time, sniffing most tenderly with her ears back—one could see her eyes closing in slow ecstasy. Then Peter barked.

We all sat up. He had cocked his ears and was standing again, nose pointing out to the garden. Harry walked quickly over to the windows. Peter looked up, squirmed, wagged his tail and sat down again looking bored. But his tail continued to thump slowly the floor.

'Don't see anything,' Harry said.

Roddy slowly withdrew his fingers from the handle of a mashie-niblick as though he had never touched it:

'Aw—Pete just wanted to break it up a bit. Hark at his old tail!'

And then Martie came in with the tea and we subsided, feeling rather foolish.

We had our tea.

After a while Harry said: 'I say, Eve *is* a long time.'

Martie made a stern face: 'Just you leave the poor mite rest. After the time she's having.'

Harry shrugged his shoulders. And then Martie went out to finish her bottling.

We poured out more and colder tea—when abruptly the house snapped alive with sound, a shot, a crash of broken glass as if glass was all over the house, for no-one knew where glass or shot was but for its great abrupt thundering presence of sound sudden in ears, inside ears, and all were on their feet and running in different directions, Barnett and Roddy to kitchen, Harry and someone like me upstairs to where that baby slept alone in the big bedroom empty of Eve.

No glass broken near baby but where was she?

And in such quiet as there was upstairs, and such peaceful order, that big sound faded and life that was upside down righted itself and a sobbing came from downstairs, a rise and fall of sighing tears like old waves of weariness. And I opened the door of a spare room to find Eve laid peacefully on the bed with a little empty brown bottle in her hand. She was cold and white and on her lips a dead and endeared smile seemed to play.

I shook her, she was like a fat heavy doll. I called at her in shocked reproachful whisper: 'Eve! Eve! Eve!' I got the bottle away and saw it had been for sleeping tablets. I put my hand in under her breast and felt for her heart—it did not seem to beat and then it did.

I was out of the room—and met Harry and Barnett and Martie coming up the stairs as if a heavy weight held them. Barnett had his arm round Martie, who was sighing like the sound of saw-music, whose face was no more than one mask of blood. 'There, there,' breathed Barnett on her, motherly, heavy with breath, 'there, there.'

'For God's sake Harry,' I shouted, 'phone an ambulance. Eve's taken an overdose.'

Harry turned his head very slowly, he gave me a dull slow look. 'Shut up,' he said, disgusted.

'For God's sake man! She's nearly done!'

He swore: 'Nonsense! She's playing. She's played that before.' His voice rose: 'How could she at a time like this!'

They were at the top of the stairs—how slowly they had climbed!—and now I got Harry's arm and tried not to shake but to grip him into sense:

'Harry—*this is serious.*'

'I'll thrash her!'

They were going to the bathroom. Barnett turned to me and said softly, surprised as though he himself were hearing it for the first time: 'A plum bottle exploded in her face. A bottle just exploded . . .'

I swung round for the big bedroom where a telephone was and shouted for an ambulance. It was a long time before an operator answered, I shouted and belled the receiver for it seemed minutes. But then a distinct voice terribly near answered and the message tightened and was in operation.

Through all this Miles slept peacefully.

Too peacefully? Suddenly shocked I went over to the cradle and took his hand in mine. It was rosy warm. He opened his eyes and gave a pleased little laugh.

When many minutes later the ambulance arrived, Harry had seen Eve and was himself white with fright. 'Damn,' he kept on saying, 'what does one *do*? Why don't we know what's best to *do*?'

For none of us, shamefully, knew anything. And there was no first-aid book in the house.

Barnett had bathed poor Martie's face, it was badly lacerated, though when the blood was momentarily gone it had no longer that first fearful look of a mask of red wet rubber.

The ambulance came and gravely, with callous skill, the attendants made Eve and Martie comfortable. Barnett and Harry went away with them.

Thus with the dogs and Roddy—and Miles—I was left alone in that house that had already quietened down. It seemed to be a house in which nothing had ever happened. We sat down among the remnants of tea and what now seemed a most stupid armoury— for those clubs and that revolver had been assembled a very long time—and simply waited. We did not talk.

The clouds lifted, and it was a beautiful evening. Once again Peter barked, and this time indeed there was a man standing alone at the open gates of the drive. His shoulders were hunched; he had about his lonely figure a certain pathos, perhaps the pathos of the hunted. But I never knew who he was, for either he went on or I turned away—by then such a man was a matter of indifference.

Miles began to cry. Roddy went up and almost instantly soothed him. The sky cast gold over everything, spiders' webs glistened like gold wire and flowers came into their own. In the great dying light even "Uplands" assumed beauty. A patting of tennis balls began to echo in the air. Harry telephoned to say that the doctors held out little hope for Eve.

I stayed down there with Harry during the next few days. An aunt of Harry's motored down and took away Miles.

It is not necessary to linger here over that distressing time. We experienced that sad great helplessness of people faced with hospitals. Everything that could be done had been done—now it only remained for the machine to do its work, the immense machine of boilers and sheets and tiled quiet business. Doctors and nurses and the porters at the door were all most considerate to our telephoning and our visits. What only was appalling in them was no reputed breeziness or cheerfulness, neither of which was shown to us—but a sense about them that as well as tending the sick, they had lives of their own. Yes, those nurses and doctors went home to lives and rooms of their own!

Poor Martie lost the sight of one eye, but otherwise her condition improved. She who had never been granted many graces—she who in fact was plain and ageing had to lose an eye. But every day Barnett travelled down with flowers and words of comfort. She was loved.

And then the day came when Eve's name was removed from the danger list. Harry and I, among a litter of bachelor tins and whisky, attempted a mild celebration in the kitchen. But it had to peter out. We went early to bed, too tired and too relieved for anything else.

Next day they telephoned to ask who George was? Her first words had been to ask for George.

For a moment Harry could not understand.

'George?' he said. 'George?'

The sister repeated: 'Yes, she keeps asking for George—little George.'

'Little . . .? Oh, the baby.'

'Baby?'

'Our little baby.'

Months later I went down to "Uplands" again. Eve was quite recovered.

Sometime after tea I was alone with her for a while. We sat relaxed in the warm bright firelight. It was a moment for reminiscence.

I remember looking over at her and smiling. One must talk of things: not leave them stored about like secrets. I remember starting to say something like: 'Well—Eve—it's good to be here again. It seems a very long time.'

She smiled too. We were at ease. 'Yes, a long time ago. And now it's all over. It's all all over.'

'No troubles?'

'None. I'm finished with all that. Never again.' She had a look of quiet composed determination. 'You know,' she went on, frowning to remember, 'it was an extraordinary feeling going away—I mean, when I took those things. I went a very long way, it seemed a thousand years. That wasn't bad, it was a long, long dream. But then they brought me back.' She shivered. 'That was the awful part. Coming back.'

She paused. Then: 'It was in a way like coming back after—after one of my, you know my whatever you call them, stories, dreams . . .'

'Mm . . .'

'Only this was a very deep dream. And the last. I think it was so deep it shocked some sense into me. At last . . .'

Then Harry came in, brisk from the cold outside, and we talked no more of it. He went over and kissed her. They looked a happy pair together in the firelight.

So there, as the facts seem to go, you have a fairly happy ending.

Eve had returned to Harry; she was shocked, for the time at least, straight.

Harry was as always in love with her. And Harry was the father of a son who was not his. But it is better not to let him know, no reason to deprive him of this his first, and most breathtaking, illusion.

I said that Eve and I talked no more. But the next day—I had stayed overnight—we did have one more word together. We were out on the lawn. It was a fine clear frosty morning. The world was crisp and certain.

But suddenly, as she smelled the air and tasted the warmth of sunlight, a distant look came into her eye.

Her mouth moved in a long-away smile. She began to speak softly: 'This weather—this always takes me back to when I was a girl, when at Christmas we used to go and stay with Uncle Hugo. He had a lovely old house, and it snowed. . . .'

'Eve!' I said. '*Eve!*'

She snapped out of it instantly. She laughed. 'Ah, well,' she said. Then to retrieve herself she turned on me sharply:

'By the way,' she said, 'I've never asked you. Do you—do you do it on a typewriter or with a, you know, a pen . . .?'

I looked her straight in her lovely eyes. This was a moment when she could be given a little of her own back.

'On a typewriter,' I lied.